THE MAN WHO DIDND'T STOP RUNNING
By: Lord Brian James

READER'S EDITION
ЭIE

Copyright © 2016 Lord Brian James

All rights reserved.

ISBN: 1523318465
ISBN-13: 978-1523318469

DEDICATION

Every last syllable of this composition is dedicated to my loving parents who continue to propel me and who were my first examples of real love. Countless times I have called you after dusk and before dawn but you have never failed at answering the phone with love. I thank you for the little 'isms' and ideologies that you've genetically passed down to me. The simple idiosyncrasies and lessons that I have relied on growing up have helped me to realize how much love you've expended to raise me properly. My career in its infant stages is filled with hundreds of false starts and failures but you never give up on me and continue to propel me to success. For that, I say thank you. My love for you will continue to flow freely like the Jordan and I will continue to be thankful for yours.

Also, this composition is dedicated to my little brother and best friend, Justin Alexander. In 1995 I prayed for a little brother and God blessed my family with such an amazing gift. Everyday, you are a constant reminder to me about the importance of guiding my steps, making sure the footprints I leave in sand can lead you in the right direction. You're on your way to becoming a man of great integrity and faith. Believe it or not, you are actually my hero and I look up to you.

Also, a huge thanks to Jillian Johnson and Gabriella Ortiz for taking the time at the end of every week during 2015 to go over this book with me. Countless minutes that you devoted to keeping my thoughts on track, you could have used that time for something else in your life. Thank you for being the firsts to believe in this dream and helping to make this possible.

Also, this composition is dedicated to my brothers of Omega Psi Phi Fraternity incorporated for introducing me to authentic perseverance. That was a lesson that made this project possible, as I have given up several moons.

CONTENTS

	Acknowledgments	i
1	The Incandescent Love	1
2	Puzzle Piece of Souls	44
3	Heroism Unheralded	84
4	Soil Of Love	119
5	An Enriching Love	146
6	Withering Roses of Love	181
7	Dusk	221
8	Dawn	252
9	Flight of the Phoenix	289
10	The Angel's Mission	322

B

CHARACTER LISTING
(Alphabetical Order ,First Name)

Adam McGaze /NBA Network Analyst & Journalist

Adam Silver/ NBA Commissioner

Alnese Alexander/Washington Post Writer

Alonzo Price/Basketball Trainer & Former UMD Athlete

Alyssa Stone/Girlfriend of UMD Star, Gerard Penny

Amber Arquette/Celebrity TV Host

Amonti Perry/Univ. of Maryland PG (2020)

Anthony Diskowski/Univ. of Marylan SG (2021)

Ashley Dennison/Rep. for OMNIVision

Austin Alonzo Arrington/Main Character

Beyonce' Knowles/Artist

Buggsy Thompkins/Univ. of Maryland Forward (2019)

Chris Broner/Agent of Gerard Penny

DaMarcus Jones/Kentucky Guard (2020)

Dante Pratt/Univ. of Maryland SF (2021)

Darius Pittman/Univ. of Maryland Center (2020)

David Pettigrew/CEO of A.M Media & Entertainment

Debbie Pettigrew/Wife of David Pettigrew

Deja Kasey Barlow-Arrington/Wife of Austin Arrington

Denise Blane/Washington Post Writer

Devin Arrington/Little Brother of Austin Arrington

Devin Whitaker/Kentucky Center (2020)

Dino McCutchen/Univ. of Maryland Athletic Director

Donn Nelson/Dallas Mavericks General Manager

Duke Michaels/Co-Host on WBLK in Buffalo

Essence Prowler/Best Friend of Deja Barlow

Gary Greeer/ESPN NBA Analyst

Lord Brian James

Gerard Penny/Univ. of Maryland Guard (2020) ;Best Friend of Austin
Dr. Hill Michaels/Primary Doctor at Doctor's Hospital
Jackson Bailey III/Kentucky Point Guard (2020)
James "Jimmy" Aaron Arrington/Brother of Austin
James Michael Arrington/Son of Austin & NFL Running Back (L.A)
Jay Z/Artist
Jefferey Dawning/Writer for Sports Illustrator
Coach Jim Donahue/Head Coach Univ. of Maryland Basketball
Lindsey Czarniak/ESPN Anchor
Mark Plummer/ESPN Radio Host
Marlon Braggs/Artist
Michael Drew IV/Univ. of Maryland Guard (2021)
Michael McDougle/Kentucky Forward (2020)
Miles Sheppard/Univ. of Maryland Guard (2021)
Nina Penny/Mother of Gerard Penny
Sin Richards/Pop Icon
Tanner Brickman/Univ. of Maryland Guard (2019)

AUTHOR'S INTRO

THANK YOU SO MUCH for embarking on this journey with me into my world. As some of you may know, I have a mammoth sized adoration for love and have become completely intoxicated on the world it can create. As a young boy, watching my parents and mentors thrive off of the inebriation of love; I quickly began to grasp the concept of caring for someone else more than myself. I became one with the ability to trust someone with my well being so deeply that I could live life on someone else's wings.

As I have been doing with my blog and other writing outlets, I will look to continue pushing the propaganda of 'the power of love'. This piece is an extension of that; One big lesson that "Love can save lives". I'm very excited about this project! It is the first part of a 4-part series designed to remind you that love can change your life. In our fast moving world we have the innate ability to succumb to the evils of society, hardening our hearts like cement in a pothole. Let this book (and series) serve as a reminder that we could use more love in life.

I sincerely do apologize for some of the language used in the dialogue between characters in the composition. Due to the desire to create a realistic environment for the story, the character's dialect is a reflection of their surroundings and mental state. Their conversation is no reflection of my personal choice of language.

Prologue

WE LOOK AT THE CLOCK on the wall and although we see time, we still don't know how much we have left. We don't know if our love is near expiration and we know not the hour nor the minute that the sun and moon will hide from us forever. I don't know how much time I have left but before the clock calls me home it's important that I pass on the most valuable lesson in life: Love.

I have been to several mountaintops in my long life. I have held up two NCAA National Championship Trophies and was drafted by the Indiana Pacers. I played 3 years of professional basketball before being struck with a career ending medical discovery and then finding another passion; Media. I am the current CEO and Founder of the world's leader in Media, ImpactComm Media. I have been on everyone's TV screens for decades and have taken over your radios for even longer. I have shared meals with some of your favorite celebrities and have been in some of the most coveted events in the world.

Out of all of these mountaintops, the highest height I have ever achieved was successfully falling in love with the Queen of my kingdom, Deja Barlow Arrington. She has taken me to places that I never imagined possible. She has shown me a side of life that I didn't know existed. She introduced myself to a better 'me' and has been by side every single step of my career. Waking up to her in my corner was the best accomplishment I have ever experienced. She has touched so many lives with her being and has shined a light on a dim

world. Chasing after her all of my life has landed me in some successful positions and she forever inspires me.

I really need you to grasp onto the ideology of falling in love; true love, and succumbing the power that it embodies.

I have no realization of how much time is left for me and I have no idea as to how many lessons I have left in me but with these downhill hours I will tell you the story of how love changed my life.

Ch. I
The Incandescent Love
1 The Revelations of Genesis

This chapter is dedicated to Buffalo, NY whose moon and dark skies provided my heart with immutable dialect and whose sunny days never let my soul leave my apartment.

January 11th, 2061

AS SHE LAY THERE, **I retracted all of the footprints that led me to her heart in the minutes prior. I thought about every rainy day that her** smile came to my rescue and remembered why I ran my entire life. Her bronze golden skin was always so vibrant and every night she would fall asleep before me, and I would take a gander at her lifeless face, my soul blinded by appreciation.

She laid in my arms many of nights before but as I look at her right now at this defining moment, I'm surrounded by emotions surrendering to both tears of joy and tears of pain as I now realize that I can't live with out her. We all have that one moment that we share with someone where we just begin to contemplate to ourselves,

"How did I get so lucky?" That was happening at this moment.

She lay on her back as she usually did, resting peacefully and sound. Every night I would wonder if I was the star of her dreams as she was the star of mine. She was such a celebrity to my soul that my subconscious was so excited to see her in my dreams, that often times I couldn't fall asleep. Yeah, she had me like that. Some nights she would fall asleep in my arms but other nights she would want to maximize her side of the bed. This was clearly one of those nights.

At this moment, I said a prayer that I will never forget, one that took every ounce of my soul:

"Father, how did I become so lucky to receive this gift? All of those nights of pain as I stare at the walls trying to figure out how to achieve my goals, all of those times I had given up and she put me on her back and dragged me to the finish line, how did I get so lucky?

[Slight cough]

I thank you for her. I thank you for every situation that led you to build this woman and place her on my path. Every ounce of her being is nothing short of a blessing and this woman, the mother of my kids and the sparkle of my eye, is the single most beneficial thing that has ever happened to my life.

She is my rock and for that I thank you. I just hope that I'm the man she needs."

I began to think about all of the accomplishments that our family had: the huge corporation, a son who is successfully playing professional football, two loving daughters who are studying for medicine and art, and her thriving influence on the female race across the country. Everything that we had accomplished couldn't have been done without her and as a man I will admit that the bridges in my life would have just been dreams if it weren't for her.

I COULD WATCH HER SLEEP FOR THE REST OF ETERNITY AS BEAUTY ENCOMPASSED HER SURFACE DAY AND NIGHT. She put up with my enormous ego and the collection of character flaws I embodied. She knocked me off of my high horse, picked me back up and taught me a lesson several times throughout our journey of love. She was my air; I knew that I would suffocate without her.

As I lay next to her I began to think about all of the things she touched, especially our home. We had just remodeled our 11,000 square foot home earlier this month. We lived in a small neighborhood right outside of Washington, DC in Howard County. The wintertime was always her time of wanting to remodel something in the home. She enjoyed hanging drapes and painting, as we would watch the driven snowfall from God's eyes. She was so happy to be prancing around the house in her hot pink sweat pants, going up and down the stairs with furniture, remodeling as she plays some vintage Beyonce'. Usually, I would be just as happy but I remember this particular time that my mind was too occupied to even be remotely involved in her remodeling fun.

"Baby, what do you think about the deep lavender with a black accent? I saw this amazing dining room set that would work perfectly in that corner too," she said to me.

Covered with disinterest and embraced by a lack of values, I responded, "It's fine honey."

She went back into the kitchen, not even responding to my emotionless reply. She had seen this before. Here's the thing: I was preparing for a company event that upcoming Friday. We were on the brink of buying one of our competitors, AM Media & Entertainment, a corporation who for years has given me a run for my money. The company's CEO, David Pettigrew, had passed away after a massive heart attack and he left the company to his wife, Debbie Pettigrew. Considering his constant stories of infidelity, she lost interest in him and his company and in her mind, he had died at the right time. She had been discussing the possibilities of selling the company to us and her sell depended solely upon our presentation that Friday night. Mrs. (Barely) Pettigrew had no interest in the company's growth and just wanted to sell it to make profit on the front end. Easy deal. I was so focused on impressing Mrs. Pettigrew that I lost sight of what was important at the time: decorating the house with my wife.

You see, I have this horrible habit of going into a zone, tunnel vision, if you will. I see the goal and nothing else, not even the ones I love. It's a problem that I have had since the beginning of time I mean, I've zoned out in every arena whether it be media or sports; consider the goal annihilated. I remember when I got my first shot at television; I forgot that anything or anyone else existed in life.

The #1 media corporation (At the time) OMNIVision, had given me a call to do red carpet interviews on national television during one of the biggest award shows, The OMNIs. I had already been doing radio in Buffalo, I was just waiting on that call for television and it happened! Everyone was going to be there, Beyonce' , Jay Z, Sin Richards, and it was going to be hosted by TV's biggest host, Amber Arquette. I was in good company!

Deja and I were a little over three years out of college (Univ. of Maryland) and my son, James, had just been born. Deja was a reporter for a local news station in Buffalo and just returned to work from maternity leave. Our conflicting schedules made us rely on each other having a good sense of responsibility and understanding when we needed each other the most. We took turns with James, some nights she would work late and myself on other nights. One night she got off early after anchoring the 4 o'clock news and I had the day off (Holiday). I had just got through cooking her favorite dinner, Lemon Pepper Shrimp with mixed vegetables, when she walked into the house.

"Dej, is that you?," I exclaimed.

"Hey honey!" she said to me with jubilation, standing on her tippy toes to get a kiss. Noticing James in his high chair at the table, she sprinted over to him doing the "Baby voice" thing and began kissing our little baby boy.

"How was it today? You didn't stutter on live TV did you?" I said to her jokingly.

"Ha – Ha (Saracasm), no you jerk," as she took off her black velvet Donna Karan jacket and threw it at me. "It actually went amazing, they asked me when will my husband be working FOR me?"

I laughed, "I know, you looked great! Glad we had that good sex last night." [Wink & the gun]

"Austin, don't talk like that around James! What is wrong with you?" she asked me.

"He has no clue what we are talking about, stop complaining and get over here," I said to her as I pulled her into my arms and began kissing her neck, trying to work out every bit of stress that tensed her muscles by using my tongue, tickling her jugular vein.

She began to giggle before hopping onto our cheap tile counter saying, "They want me to anchor the morning show on Thursday.... I'm so excited and nervous!"

I could tell that she needed this time of "relaxation", I could hear the soothe in her voice, "You know I can get used to this, working all day coming home to my man cooking my favorite meal."

"I bet you can. [Pause for sucking on neck] But I'm back to work tomorrow," I said to her.

She pulled her neck away, looked at me and then gave me a kiss on the lips and hopped off of the counter, walked to the cabinets grabbing plates and utensils. As she began making our plates, my phone rang. I reached in my pocket and picked up my phone to see that it was a number that wasn't saved in my phone, area code (310).

"I hate unknown numbers, I don't even feel like being bothered," I said out loud.

'You should answer it, you never know what it could be baby," she replied.

I smirked at her but just for shits and giggles, I answered the call:

"Hello."

"Hi, is this Austin Arrington?" the voice on the phone replied.

"Yeah, this is him, who is this?" I said.

She replied, "This is Ashley from OMNIvision, we have been trying to reach you. You have a minute?"

I replied with confidence and excitement, "Yeah, I can talk. Wassup?"

She continued, "We want you to do some freelance work for our OMNIs award show this year, we are…….." the rest was a blur.

ONCE I HEARD THE FOCAL POINT OF THE CONVERSATION, I MENTALLY BEGAN PREPARING MYSELF

FOR THE BIGGEST OPPORTUNITY OF MY LIFE.

I had already mentally packed my bags and was on the plane heading to the west coast. I saw myself on the red carpet with all the big name celebrities; I saw myself on TV, and I could almost taste the success.

"Mr. Arrington…. Mr. Arrington are you there? We said we would need to put you on a flight immediately, is that going to be a problem?," Ashley asked.

Without hesitation or in my case, consideration I responded, "No ma'am not a problem at all, I'll see you in a little while."

"Great. We'll have you on the 9:10 flight to LAX tonight." She affirmed.

I pressed the red button on my iPhone while trying to keep composure.

Deja was sucking the Lemon Pepper off of her fingers after grabbing another piece of shrimp out of the pot, "Who was that baby?"

With complete disbelief and shock I replied, "That was OMNIvision, they want me to come to LA for the

OMNIs! I'll be on the red carpet doing interviews!"

She dropped her plate and ran over to me, "Oh my God baby that is so good!! I'm so happy for you!! This is amazing, we have to go and pick out an outfit tomorrow! You know what, I'll call out sick, I'm just doing production tomorrow night anyway."

I was excited but quickly calmed down as I realized that my next few sentences were going to cause a volcanic eruption in Deja's mind. Walking over to her as she picks up her phone to call her head producer, I touched her wrist saying, "They want me to leave tonight."

She turned to me as if she was completely disgusted, "But Austin, you know Thursday is a big day for me...."

I tried to interject but we began talking over each other, "I know honey, but this is the big opportunity that we both have been praying for, you know how bad I want this. You know how bad we want this for us!"

She continued, "Thursday is a big day for me and even if you couldn't find time in your busy schedule to watch your wife anchor her first morning show…"

I tried to interject again but she just got louder to finish her sentence, "YOU COULD AT LEAST FUCKING TAKE CARE OF OUR SON!"

James started to scream.

She was a little lady with so much patience but when there was an earthquake strong enough to awaken her volcano, she would erupt with arguably the hottest lava known to man. Once she erupted, silence was your best bet.

She grabbed James out of his high chair and angrily walked off to our guest room slamming the door loud enough to knock a picture of my parents off of the wall.

Now here's the kicker and the tunnel vision I warned you of earlier; I knew I should have cared. I knew that she had a point and that I was being selfish. I knew that her biggest day was coming up in two days and she would need me to be there for her to support her and to make sure that our newborn son was taken care of. We weren't from here and had no one of proven valor that we trusted to watch our son; we were supposed to be there for each other when things like this happen. I knew how I was supposed to react, I should have told OMNIvision that I can't make it until Friday, but I just didn't care. I didn't care about anything but the prize: that's tunnel vision.

I rummaged through our small 3-bedroom apartment in Allentown near downtown Buffalo. I packed two bags, and called a cab to take me to the airport. Before walking out, I knocked on the door to tell Deja goodbye but at this point in time, she could care less if the plane went down or if I got in an accident on the way to the airport. Never opening the door, I said to her, "Deja honey, I'm sorry but I have to go. I love you and I'll see you Monday."

That cab ride was the longest. I contemplated asking the driver to turn around, I even asked him for some advice but to no avail. He didn't care about anything but cash or credit card. I expected my phone to ring. I expected her to call me saying that she is sorry and that she loves me, wishing me well but none of that happened. In fact, that entire week we didn't talk.

I called her after live streaming her phenomenal show on that Thursday. I mean, she did an outstanding job. My Queen made me proud but she never called back. I don't even know if she watched me at the OMNIs on Sunday.

My plane landed back in Buffalo at 11:16 on Monday morning, 3 hours late because of a huge snowstorm (Nothing new). When I got off that plane, I honestly didn't know what to expect. I was hoping to walk out of the airport and see my beautiful bride sitting behind the wheel, with the seat pushing her up against the steering wheel. I expected to see her staring out the window waiting for her knight in shining armor to walk out but none of that happened. In fact, when I landed I realized that I wasn't her knight in shining armor but more like her disgrace of a husband.

I called one of my Co-Hosts, Duke Michaels, to come pick me up in his Suburban. It took him nearly 30 minutes to get here and it was the extra time that I needed to mentally prepare myself for "Hurricane Deja" when I finally got home. Duke finally pulls up in his matte black suburban, I hop in and the confessional almost immediately begins:

"So how did it go man? Any good news?" Duke says to me.
I wanted to be joyous but even the amazing news I had about the OMNIs wasn't enough sunshine to brighten up my world without Deja. I said to Duke, "Yeah man, it went great. They want me to report from New York City a couple times a week and cover their big events happening in the city."

"You don't sound excited," he responded in a confused manor. "Something must have happened between you and D." I ended up telling him the entire story without leaving out a single detail.

Duke has been one of my good friends for years. We started radio together in D.C before getting the offer to take the show on the road to Buffalo. We now broadcast in 7 cities! Working together for so long has allowed me to see that the Duke is about one thing: Honesty.

"Listen man, you have to stop being about yourself. It was a great opportunity on the West Coast I agree but, you have to remember there are two people in the marriage and two careers to cater to," he remarked.

The guilt began to sink into my soul, suffocating my ego by the neck. Duke's honesty has always been a painful pleasure but in this situation his words may have literally been the saving grace to my marriage and my life.

We pulled up to my building and as I'm getting out of his truck he says to me, "DON'T YOU LOSE THAT GIRL. ONLY A FOOL MISPLACES A DIAMOND."

Those words resonated with my soul incessantly. I grabbed my bags off of the back seat and began to walk towards the door. Deja's car was on the street so I knew that she was in the apartment. Feeling guilty and confused I tried to find the words to say once I see my darling bride. The Duke had me scared thinking that I could lose my lady and at that moment I realized that she was truly my world. Don't get me wrong, I knew this before but I really experienced it as I walked up the stairs of our building.

I opened our door to a dark apartment and the whispers of her favorite movie, Titanic, in the background. The house smelled of air freshener and there was not a pile of junk anywhere. Our front door walks directly into the kitchen and the family room was in the far back of the apartment with a hall off to the right leading to the bedrooms. I stood in the spotless kitchen and stared into the family room to see the top of her head hunched to the side as if she had fallen asleep. Trying not to wake her (Because I'm already on her bad side), I gently placed my keys on the table and began heading towards the family room.

Duke's words still resonating in my mind, I get closer and closer to my beautiful bride. As I reach in closer, I notice an image that I will never forget. An image that changed my life because it was a reminder of how important it is for me to be a good man for my family. I saw this beautiful image that I could have framed, Deja was sleeping soundly with our baby boy, James, in her arms. The two of them looked like a sculpture, created by God himself with the highest form of artistry; a sculpture that radiated true love.

I didn't know exactly what to do but I knew that whatever happened between Deja and me, I was going to make it right. I knew that I had too much to lose at this point and I did not want to see my Queen on another man's chessboard. I knew that I was going to make it right for my family. It didn't take my University of Maryland degree to figure that out either. All it took was a little common sense stuffed with a lot of humility. Love was in the air and if I never truly contracted the bug before, I was surely "love sick" now. I sat on our leather sectional next to Deja and pulled the two of them into my arms. We all fell asleep together with the TV on low and the lights off as we became one with the falling snow outside of our 3rd story window.

3 hours had passed and James had decided he was done sleeping. He began crying with the volume on 10 and Deja quickly jumped up to try and calm our little boy down.

"Shhhh… It's ok baby, Mama's got you…" she said to him as she began pacing the family room floor. Still a little bit nervous for the conversation that awaits us, I sat there in silence, as I feared that I didn't confidently know the words to say to her. Being the bigger and better person than me she finally broke the awkward silence, "Little Jimmy is hungry! (In her baby voice)," turning to me and said, "Go into the pantry and grab the Apricots, Aus." I hopped up like a soldier in the army, grabbed the Apricots and brought them to her.

We sat in the family room feeding our seed and I just couldn't stop staring at the two. I kept replaying Duke's words of wisdom and I finally un-tucked my dick from between my legs and spoke up to my bride, "Deja honey, listen."

She could sense that I was about to attempt to reconcile and that she would need her full attention. She turned her body so that she was completely facing me and she was ready for me to say what I had to say.

"Please just listen, I want to get this off of my chest," I pleaded to her. She nodded her head and I continued, "What I did was completely wrong and selfish of me and I am sorry. I look at you and my little king (rubbing James' head) and I realized that this isn't about just me anymore. My entire week was hell without you, and even though I was speaking to an entire world of people, it didn't feel the same without you. I'm going to get myself together, I'm going to be a better man and we are going to be unstoppable."

(I had no idea where these words were coming from by the way).

"From now on, I will always put the family first even if that means biting the bullet on an opportunity of a lifetime [sarcastically]. I finally realized that you two are all I would ever need in this life and I will never leave you again baby please forgive me [begging]."

She smirked, "You promise?"

I responded, "Yes, I promise baby I can't do anything without you. My world and entire being is ….."

She cut me off, "Ok, ok please stop you're making me sick Austin. I forgive you, damn." She began to laugh and I began to breathe easily as my world slowly returned to its axis.

"But I should leave you for wearing that ugly tie on TV, I see why you need me," she said to me.

Although she low key insulted me, a jab never felt so good. I was glad to have my lady back and I was glad that God gave me a second chance at being a father and husband. In reality, I could have lost my wife that day out of my selfishness and lust for success. MY WORLD WOULD HAVE SURELY CRUMBLED AND I WOULDN'T BE HERE TODAY IF SHE DID NOT FORGIVE ME THAT DAY.

Much like any other apology, the sentiments are temporary. I never was that selfish and disrespectful again but I did make some of those same mistakes over and over again. A couple of times since that situation, she has had to reprimand me for putting my family on the back burner. She would call me out and then I would straighten up but as we got older, she would just go on about her business, with or without me.

Often times I would have to remind myself that time with each other is precious and that tomorrow has no assurance. As I lay here next to her peacefully resting, seemingly lifeless, I regret every minute with her that I forfeited to work. I didn't feel bad about my disengagement in her annual remodeling fun until now. I actually wanted to wake her up and go remodel the home now just to try and make up for lost time. NO MATTER HOW REGRETFUL YESTERDAY IS, DESTINATIONS ARE ONLY CONCERNED WITH THE MILES AHEAD AND THE PATHS YOU TAKE TO GET THERE. As morbid as this may sound, death is our only guaranteed destination and with that being said the rest of this ride has to be fun.

I GRABBED HER HAND SO TIGHTLY THAT I WANTED TO GRIP HER SOUL. I wanted the skin on skin contact to make the sun rise in her subconscious, warming her spirit to make her smile feel comfortable. I grabbed her, while she was in a deep sleep and pulled her even closer to me before kissing her on the forehead.

Holding her in my arms never felt so real. I stared down at her, sleeping so peacefully and it all just hit me; this woman is everything that I'm not and every single day since we first met has been the best day of my life.

I began to think about the day our paths crossed.

Chapter II
Puzzle Piece of Souls
2 Harmony of Attraction

This chapter is dedicated to Buffalo, NY whose moon and dark skies provided my heart with immutable dialect and whose sunny days never let my soul leave my apartment.

March 9th, 2020

WE WERE BOTH sophomores when we met; it was early March because I specifically remember that awkward transitional weather from Winter to spring.

I was a partial-scholarship athlete, playing basketball for the Terrapins. I didn't get much playing time though, My earlier years, I was more a practice player than anything but it was definitely a great experience so I never left the team. I remember we had just wrapped up a tough practice after suffering a terrible loss to Michigan State the night before.

Michigan State had been the team to beat that year and ironically they were in our conference. Our team was slated to be one of the best Terrapin teams in the history of University of Maryland basketball. High expectations from both teams birthed a "Rivalry" of sorts and also set the stage for one of the most memorable games in the history of college basketball.

We went into 3 overtimes with the Spartans, fighting for the #1 spot in the Big 10. One of my best friends and team mates, Gerard 'GP' Penny, led us through one of our toughest match ups ever. After having an amazing game he fell short on the last shot in the 3rd OT, missing the tying free throw with 0.4 on the clock. Needless to say we took that loss hard and our coach took it the toughest, repaying us with a tough practice the next day.

Laps, gases, and full speed

scrimmages dominated our 3 hour practice that Wednesday night. Along with the smell of sweat and defeat, the air was filled with a horrible energy. An energy of anger, disappointment and resentment. This was easily the most unwelcoming practice for the press to join; this kind of energy was built for only the strongest of journalists.

The clock struck 9:17 (pm) and coach yelled, "Alright, we're done here," as he briskly exited the Comcast Center.

My team mates were so gassed , most of them just took a seat on the shiny hardwood floor, a few even laid down. I think we expected an apology from coach for running us so hard but he wasn't even around. I sat near half court, barely alive but little did I know, I was minutes away from meeting someone who would change my life forever.

Although we dropped like flies after practice, the media was still relentless. After losing such a tough game, they each swarmed us, trying to get one of us to say something about our loss and put our coach in jeopardy or bash our team mates. They stamped the court the minute coach walked out of the door and all I could think was 'Good Luck' to them. I looked into

GP's eyes and could tell that he was not there mentally. I could tell that my friend was truly going through a storm mentally after the media turned him from a hero to a villain, blaming our loss on him. I knew that much of the media was there to talk to him and I knew that he was going to explode.

As the reporters stormed him he began to yell, "Don't fucking walk over here and don't ask me anything." I dropped my head because my best friend's anger issues were surely going to get him in trouble and I knew that.

He continued, "You should be

ashamed of yourself. You ruined my life and now you fucking want me to save yours? You're fucking bitches and I hope all of you lose your jobs. I'm one of the best to ever do it, don't you ever fucking disrespect me like that."

He began to charge back at the reporters and we could tell that the reporters were fearful, not knowing if he was going to throw a punch at them. A few teammates and myself ran to help restrain GP as he continued yelling. He was yelling so loud that Coach Donahue walked back into the gym and immediately shut down press. He dragged GP out of the gym and much of the press followed but one beautiful, young looking lady.

I LOOKED INTO THE STANDS AND SAW THIS GOLDEN SKINNED BEAUTY SLOWLY PACKING UP HER EQUIPMENT. She turned her head and kind of flipped her bang, revealing her tearful eyes, which immediately caught my attention.

I approached her, "Wassup little lady? Is everything ok?"

She sniffled and turned her head hiding, her eyes and trying to conceal the fact that she was wiping her eyes. She responded, "Yes, I'm fine just packing up to get out of here."

I was usually a shy fellow, well, not really shy just more reserved but for some reason, confidence overtook my soul. I reached and grabbed her arm preventing her from continuing to pack up her recording equipment. She was shocked and frozen as my confidence caused a hurricane in her world.

"Look at me," I said. She locked her eyes on mine, as her pink eyes look as if they drowned in the Chesapeake Bay. She looked away in discomfort before finally opening her heart, "It's just that, I was sent here by my teacher as a make up assignment, to save my grade."

I looked down at this angelic little lady, "Ok what's wrong?"

She continued, "I was supposed to grab an interview from one of your teammates , just to talk about...."

AT THIS POINT I REALIZED I COULD SAVE HER DAY. Anyone staring into her eyes would have been trying to put on a cape for her world as well. I stopped her mid sentence, "Unpack your stuff."

She looked at me confused, stopping her conversation, "Huh?....

Why?" she said.

Coach walked back in with anger written all over his face. Dealing with GP was always a headache, I could just imagine what type of trouble he may have caused Coach. He looked in our direction and yelled, 'If you are press then please get the hell out of my gym."

This young lady looked so scared and stuck, I could tell she was young as her discomfort revealed her age. I spoke up to coach, "She's with me coach." He rolled his eyes and walked out of the gym. The rest of the players had already cleared the gym and it was just me and this beautiful stranger. She stood there kind of in shock, still confused as to if I was the superman of her life right now.

"Does it always take you this long to unpack your equipment for interviews? You should work on that," I said to her.

She smiled and brokenly replied, "You're.... You're going to give me the interview?"

I laughed and threw her one of our shooting shirts, "Wipe your eyes, put a smile on. Yes, I'm going to try and salvage your grade."

PUTTING ON THE CAPE THAT DAY WOULD PAN OUT TO BE

THE BEST DECISION OF MY LIFE.

"Before we start, let me interview you first," I said to her as she scribbled in her journal. She smiled at me, "Ok."

I asked her, "Do you even know my name?"

I was a highly recruited High school point guard out of DeMatha Catholic High School but my coach hasn't given me my time to shine here yet. I barely played in the beginning of my career, but I knew my time was coming in the next year or so. After not being given much opportunity to show that I was talented on the court, I knew that a lot of people had probably forgotten about me. Apparently, this stranger was not one of the ones who forgot me.

She surprisingly replied, "Yes. Austin Arrington. I remember you from the Ohio State game."

However, I did have one claim to fame so far. In the beginning of my freshman season, our star senior point guard Miles Shepherd, tore his ACL against Ohio State . His replacement was a speedy white boy, also a senior, Tanner Brickman. Tanner had a horrible habit of playing defense with his hands, often times getting himself in foul trouble. In our first meeting against Ohio State, Tanner had got himself in the usual foul trouble but this time it was literally the worst time possible. His speed gave us an edge against Ohio State and kept us close with the top team in the nation, The Buckeyes.

Tanner then got his fifth and final foul, getting him ejected from the tight game with 2:31 left on the clock.

"Arrington. Let's go," Coach Donahue yelled down the bench. I jumped up with excitement, enthusiasm and focus. "Keep us in the game Aus, don't fuck this up. GP will strike, we just need you to protect the rock," coach told me as I walked to the table to check into the game.

As I walked into the game, I felt chills as I looked up at the jumbotron, watching myself walk onto the court. GP nodded to me, "Just like old times bro, let's handle this work." GP was also a highly recruited guard out of the DC area but he went to Bishop O'Connell High School. Before splitting up for high school, we had played together since kindergarten in different Rec Leagues and AAU Tournaments.

Tanner's foul put their (Ohio State's) star guard on the free throw line. He nailed the two shots giving them a 5-point lead. GP inbounded the ball to me and I immediately came alive. I led a 5 point comeback in nearly 2 minutes. Then, GP started going back and forth with one of their forwards and put us in a situation where we were looking at a tie ball game with :22 seconds on the clock.

GP passed the ball in and they intentionally fouled me to put me on the free throw line. I nailed both shots, putting us in the lead with about :20 seconds on the clock. We were in a Full Court Press (We called it 'Omaha'). Coach Donahue yelled from the sidelines, "Protect this house fellas!"

They tried inbounding the ball but ended up giving me the break of my life. I intercepted the ball and they intentionally fouled me putting me back on the free throw line.

I nailed both shots again putting us up 4 points against the #1 Ohio State Buckeyes. We locked down defensively once again, solidifying our win. Easily the best night in my life but in a fast moving world, I know a lot of people had forgotten about that epic night.

She didn't forget it though.

"Wow, you remember that night?" I

asked her.

"Yes, of course. You saved us that day," she responded., "But do you know my name?"

"I was going to get to that," I said. "Tell me what it starts with and I'll guess." I was a corny guy who still loved to play corny games with the women, one of which was guessing their names.

"It's start with a D," she said.

(I had a great 'That's what she said' joke but concealed it for obvious reasons).

I guessed everything but her name and finally she told me that her name was 'Deja'.

LITTLE DID I KNOW THAT THIS IS A NAME THAT WOULD REMAIN IN MY LIFE FOREVER.

"That's a dope name," I said to her.

You know that awkward point in love movies where the two main characters lock eyes and have a "moment"? Yeah, that happened. It was the first time I was suffocated by her smile and trapped by her eyes; a "playa's" worst nightmare. This split second of eye contact alerted my subconscious that I would have to grow up soon.

[Awkward silence]

After the longest 4 seconds known to man, she broke the silence by proceeding, "So my report has to be on an athlete but can't be about sports…"

Sarcastically, I interrupted, "Jesus, that makes sense….."

She continued, "Yeah, I know but that just means I have to ask the fun and nosy questions so I hope you're ready."

LITTLE DID SHE KNOW THAT SHE HAD ALREADY

CAPTURED MY HEART AND MIND, THE GLOW IN HER EYES CREATING A PRISON FOR MY MIND; I was under her control and she could have asked me anything from the size of my penis to my social security number and I wouldn't panic even after she ran off with my money.

Snickering I replied, "Sure, let's get it!"

"Besides going pro, what are some of your goals and aspirations?" she asked me. I knew that was going to be the first question because something in the energy told me that she wasn't so much concerned with sports; Little did she know we have more in common than she was aware of.

"Well, I honestly don't really want to go pro," I said to her. She looked at me with a piercing and confusing glance as I continued, "I would much rather work on my media career and start saving up for my media company…. Who knows, I may hire you."

Once again, my corny "one-liner" went completely unengaged, as something else seemed to grab her attention. Til' this day, I think that moment was when she fell in love with me. She realized that we are turned on by the same details in the world; it's like an artist realizing the connection to another artist by using the same colors. It was her first peak at my pallet and her first peak at the canvas. We both were painting the same picture.

"Hire me huh? That's cute…. Ok so, where do you see yourself in 6 years?" She responded.

Somehow, that one statement took me on journey through my childhood watching my parents and their random acts of love throughout our house. My parents were like newlyweds and they were the best example possible of true love for me and my little brother, Jimmy. They woke up everyday falling in love with each other even more than the day before. They did everything they could to keep our family together, reminding us that there is nothing more important than having each other.

I answered her question, "I see myself married to the woman who will take my soul." I don't think she was expecting such a vibrating answer. I continued, "I see myself cutting the ribbon on the first portion of my media company, holding my pregnant wife's hand as she stands beside me boldly, making me feel warm in a cold world."

It was very Shakespeare-esque I know, but I meant every word. I really had dreams deeper than the basketball court. In the locker room, we would joke about all of the girls that we were sleeping with and we would always have celebratory conversations about exploring our "singleness". My teammates would laugh telling their jokes and I constantly was left out because I didn't like that lifestyle. I was the lover at heart who would rather have a strong woman by his side, than a choice of many weak ones. I always dreamed of love; Like cupid fell asleep drunk, the images were endless.

I SAW THE BEAUTY IN LOVE

and felt the strength of it because my parents always were great examples of it. It was a strength that I yearned for, my soul was dying without it and when she asked that question, I think she could feel the gravity of my thirst for love.

"Wow, that's deep," she exclaimed. "I never expected that from you Loverboy, I thought all you ball players were the same."

I replied, "That's what you get for categorizing me with 'All the ball players', now you know what you're dealing with."

"Cool, well it was just two questions, thank you for your...." She continued as she began breaking down her college student media equipment. I stopped her as she was unzipping her microphone bag, "Wait, I have two questions for you too."

The look on her face told me that she was happy that this wasn't over. I didn't want it to be over either. Usually I'm shy and very reserved but something over took my spirit and I decided that I was going to try my hand with her.

"Ok, let's have it Mr. Arrington," she said to me. I asked, "Do you like fried chicken?" She looked at me with the most puzzled and confused look as she started to grin a little bit, "Yes, I do...."

Trust me, I know what I'm doing. Our campus in College Park was known for various food attractions but one of the best late night spots was Royal Farms Chicken on Route 1, where God himself cooks the chicken. Usually after practice, our team would go grab some chicken and snacks but since today's practice went horrible, I'm here by myself. I figured that my new acquaintance and future wife would love to go and grab some late night chicken.

"That leads to my next question; Would you like to take a walk to go get some Royal Farms?" I asked her. I could tell she thought that my slick way of asking her on a cheap date turned her on. She cracked a smile and continued to pack her equipment, "Ok but you're carrying the bags."

That was a deal I didn't mind making because she was a book that I wanted to finish reading. I knew that more time with her would help silence everything going on in my life. I had just met my hero and God had just introduced me to my angel. I picked up her bags, and grabbed my shooting shirt and we headed for the door.

As we were walking out, GP was heading out of the locker room on the east side of the gym. His head hanging low because of the commotion earlier, the look of defeat on his face worried me. I wasn't the only one who noticed, Deja said to me, "I think you should go say something to your friend." I really wanted to make sure GP was ok but I also really wanted to take this beautiful young lady on this really cheap, college-styled date to Royal Farms. "At least make sure he is ok," she said to me.

I looked into her eyes and felt the gravity of her command as the compassion she had in her heart was written all over her facial expression. It was a chilling and stern look, one that you couldn't disappoint but couldn't help but love. I replied, "Ok, give me two seconds," desperate for whatever God had planned for the two of us, I exclaimed, " Please don't go anywhere."

She smiled and nodded.

Her halo was definitely ever-present because what GP needed right then and there was me. Somehow, she knew that and knew how upside down his world was right now. She knew nothing about him off the court, nothing about his family or any of the mental battles he fights. Very few know that he watched his father abuse his mother when he was younger. Only I knew the trepidation it caused this young man and only I knew that when his anger explodes, it's not really him. It's all of the pain and anger built up over the years exploding at once. You can only cover a wound for so long without suture; even volcanoes need relief.

More importantly, only I knew that Gerard had started seeing a psychiatrist twice a week and had been diagnosed with a bi-polar disorder. The doctor said that GP's mind state was completely unstable and even asked that he take time off and away from the team and spotlight because she feared for the time when the volcano would erupt. Much like it did a few hours ago.

She smiled and nodded.

GP was headed for the door out of the dimly lit gym when he just stopped, leaning his head up against the wall as he broke down. I quickly shifted from a slower paced walk to a brisk jog as I noticed my "Ace" in distress. I didn't say anything, I just pulled his shoulder and pulled him toward me and he cried on my shoulder. His world was completely crushed. Everything that he had been fighting in his life, all of his demons were dancing on my shoulders as tears of pain and sorrow. I looked over at Deja and she clutched her hands across her mouth and even from a distance, I could see her eyes start to water up. She sat down on the bottom bleacher as she patiently waited for me to console my best friend.

His pain quickly turned to rage as he looked up and pushed me away. "GP," I mumbled to him.

"Na dog, why they doing me like this? We one of the top teams in the nation, I'm one of the top players in the world and this how they treat me? Fuck I do to them bruh? HUH? Rings bro, RINGS…. That's what we do around here and you know how they repay us? That's how they repay me? I'M THE BAD GUY," he yelled at me furiously. His eyes were blood shot red and the veins in his neck were popping out; He had the face of Satan.

"G, calm down… You're not the enemy bruh… Let's just go chill," I said to him in a calming voice. Neither my tone nor choice of words was enough to keep Satan in chains, "Na Austin… I'm going to tell you what I'm going to do," he said to me.

Now don't get me wrong I love this man to death, this is my best friend but, with that being said, I know when to hold em' and when to fold em'. My hand was empty.

He continued, "I'm going to get the fuck out of this gym, go into my dorm and crack this fifth of Henny (Hennessey) until I can't keep my eyes open."

"Man that ain't going to solve nothing, go get some rest and get ready-" I replied to him. He didn't like my response and where I was headed so he cut me off, "Nah, I told you what I'm going to do and if you were really my mans you would leave me the fuck alone."

As he said his final words, I kind of hung my head in defeat because I had seen this before. He had reacted like this before and there isn't anything I can do about this. He developed a horrible habit of running to the bottle whenever the waves in his life grew unbearable. It hurt to see him beat himself up but nothing hurts worse than bad timing. I'm just waiting on the right time to really talk to him about his problem. Now was not the right time.

He marched sternly out of the gym, you could hear the anger in his footsteps. I turned around to go get Deja as she hopped up off of the bleacher wiping her eyes, "You alright?" I asked her as she walked my way. She nodded 'yes' as she reached out for a hug. "Now let's go eat," I said to her and we proceeded to our first date; Royal Farms. 8 pieces of chicken for $5.29, it gets no better.

THAT NIGHT I FELT HER ANGELIC SOUL AS SHE ENCOURAGED ME TO CONSOLE MY FRIEND. I felt the beauty within her as she allowed her good spirit to campaign for my soul. The best part of it all is that this is only the beginning.

As my sophomore season finished

out, Coach began to give me more minutes. We were eliminated out of the National Tournament that year in the Sweet 16. Ending that season as a player in the rotation, I was looking forward to my upcoming Junior year season.

Deja was there every step of the way as we began dating. She helped me see that if I wanted more playing time, I would have to go get it. I was months away from finding out that she brings out the best in me.

Chapter III

Heroism Unheralded

3 Kissed By An Angel

This chapter is dedicated to Indianapolis, a city who was nice enough to stand at the end of the dark tunnel, swinging a dim lamp.

December 16th 2020

MY JUNIOR YEAR season was still fresh and although the hope was still there, my spirit was a little bit crushed. My minutes had decreased significantly thanks to a freshman point guard from Audenried High School in Philadelphia, Amonti Perry. He was 2 inches taller than me with a skinny frame and although I was quicker than him, he was stronger when driving to the rim because he was an aggressive ball player. I will be a man and admit that I felt threatened.

Even though life on the court was painful, Deja' had found a way to make herself my haven of happiness. I grew fond of her stern but loving tone and vibrant personality, learning to trust her every word. She led me through many dark tunnels and gave me the courage to walk in the dark shadows of the unknown. 10 months flew by but everyday with her was a blessing. It felt like everyday was Christmas and under the tree was everything I ever wanted. She brought out the best of me, and that was for sure.

That semester, she began her active internship as our media student coordinator and reporter for Terps Basketball. In other words, we got to see a lot of each other and she got to witness first hand the frustration I was feeling after losing my starting spot to a freshman. I think watching her boyfriend suffer on the bench drained her so much that she couldn't enjoy her new ventures in her career. All summer she talked about her excitement and hopes of getting this internship but, I was being such a baby that my dark days clouded her sunshine. It hurt her to have to write about the decline of her boyfriend. Then, everything blew up and she completely abandoned her journalist mode.

You see, we had to play a big, out-of-conference game in 4 days and coach was running a high intensity scrimmage between the 1s (First Teamers) and 2s (Second Teamers). The season had just started and he knew we needed an extra kick in the ass to be able to run with the No.7 Texas Longhorns. Considering the fact that I lost my spot to a freshman (Still a little salty about that), I was normally the 'bread-winner' of the Second Teamers. Whenever we scrimmaged, I was the one guarding Amonti Perry no matter the situation.

He had a great skill set, although it hasn't quite matured all the way. His potential and youth were his strong points with the coaching staff but I made it my mission every practice to expose his weakness; his youth. I would get inside his head and try to make him explode on the court. He had a great sense of athleticism but a horrible poker face. Play after play, he would let me get inside of his emotions, shaking the comfort in his world which ultimately began to hinder his skillset.

It was filthy of me but it had to be done because coach had to see that I was the better choice to start at the point guard position. I knew what I was doing. I knew that I could make him a bad basketball player just by using a few words, I knew that I could prove that he was weak.

This scrimmage got out of hand quickly as the focus shifted from preparing for Texas to literally a small battle between me and

Amonti. He would drive the lane throwing elbows and I would get him right back on the other end of the court. One particular play, he didn't even dribble the ball. He was completely out of the game and focused solely on his battle with me. I was coming off of a double team as the first teamers shifted the ball back in the hands of Amonti. He caught the ball and then stared at me with anger and frustration in his bloodshot eyes as he began to drive the lane.

I knew coach was watching closely and I knew that I could prove to him that Amonti was not ready to be the star of this team. He began charging the lane and as he got closer, I planted my feet and prepared to take the hardest charge in the history of college basketball. He was like a runaway train; his aggression made him almost a completely unstoppable force. He ran me over as if I didn't exist and I fell hard to the ground.

The whistle blew, " Amonti, what the hell?" Coach yelled.

I interjected with some sarcastic advice for Amonti, "Control yourself young fella.... That's a charge playa."

He responded in his Philadelphia rhetoric and tone, "Get the fuck out of my way then old bul." Coach pointed out the salient issue, Perry didn't even dribble the ball. He literally just wanted to drive the lane and run me over. His emotions got the best of him and everybody finally saw his weakness- but things would get worse.

Tension covered the air in our gym as our team mates began trying to calm us down but I could look over at the young point guard's face and tell that things were about to get crazy.

"I'm the best out here, he don't want no problems with me. I'll end it all for him right now, " Amonti yelled to everyone as some of our teammates continuously tried to hold him back. I stood under the basket as they stood near the free throw line, I watched Amonti erupt. The bigger issue with our team was that with the addition of the young diva Amonti, we now have two divas because my best friend GP has forever been the diva of the team and needless to say, he was not going to sit back and watch this happen. Gerard charged over to where Amonti was arguing and swung on the young Point Guard, erupting the gym into a brawl. Amonti fell to the ground after that powerful blow to head and players began to take sides as the arguments continued. One of the Freshman big men, Darius Pittman, blind-sided GP with a crushing blow to the jaw.

I stood under the basket in complete disbelief of the turmoil that I caused my team. I was just trying to prove a point to a young warrior that he needed to humble himself before God knocked him off of his horse; I didn't mean to play God. My entire team was fighting and I was just standing there. I even watched my coach, Jim Donahue try and break up this fight between some of the biggest players in the nation. Coach was a small white man from suburban New Hampshire; breaking up fights between guys from the hood was not his specialty.

Grunting and explicatives filled the air along with the sounds of thousands of shutter flashes as press and media began to report on this moment in history, a moment that they began to refer to as "The Brawl At College Park". There was a pool of blood on the floor where Amonti had fallen and GP had been completely knocked out and laid on the floor. Coach finally got the players separated and tried to calm everyone down. Darius looked over at Amonti, "You good?" Amonti didn't respond, grabbing his jaw as blood leaked from his nose. Medics were trying to tend to his injuries but the young and fiery point guard stormed out of the gym dripping blood all the way to the exit.

I looked over near the right side of the half court line where GP was still laid out, the medics were trying to wake him up as well. Darius Pittman was a 7 foot 1, 342 pound, 19 year old Freshman from New Jersey; his punches surely packed some power. His punch was enough to knock our star player completely unconscious. His punch was enough to get me to realize so many fallacies in my personality and helped me understand the gravity of my selfishness and how everything was my fault. Coach Donahue was tending to GP (along with the medics) and I just stood there looking around the gym in complete disbelief about what my team had just gone through.

The athletic director and former Terrapin, Dino McCutchen, stormed into the gym confused as to what had taken place here. He was a football legend here at University of Maryland and played 13 seasons for the New York Giants going down in history as one of the best linebackers to play the game. He was actually from Brooklyn and still carried his heavy northeastern demeanor and accent. In the most stern and unpleasant tone he dismissed every member of the press, "If you are not a member of the

University of Maryland staff then get out of my gym. As the facilitator of this property, any photo or video that you captured cannot be used from today. You have 3 minutes to pack up all of your belongings before I notify the authorities that you are trespassing. Get the fuck out and get out quick." We as a team knew that whenever Dino got involved, things were serious. Dino was the one guy who got GP to focus last year by threatening to sit him down the entire season. After their conversation, GP brought his grades up an entire grade marking and those of us who were close to him noticed a change in his personality; Dino changed his life.

As the press began to exit the gym (in fear), I glanced over at my last but loyal fan, Deja. She was still sitting there in complete shock at the events that just took place; I don't think any one saw this coming. I knew that she was utterly disappointed in me because she gave me a look that said, "This is your fault."

Dino's deep voice bellowed, "You... Are you working right now?" pointing at Deja. I uttered the first words I've said in 15 minutes, "Yeah, she is with the team coach." She looked over at me obviously still disgusted and said, "You know what? I think I am going to go." Dino replied, "Well go ahead now before the medics get here young lady."

I WAS SCARED BECAUSE I THOUGHT SHE HAD SEEN THE

WORST OF ME AND OPTED AGAINST DEALING WITH ME ANY LONGER.

I thought she had seen the evil side of me and decided that it wasn't what she wanted to be in a relationship with. I walked over to her as she packed up her stuff, "Deja, honey wait…." She quickly replied, "Don't speak to me Austin, I don't know who you are right now." She zipped up her bag and dashed for the door as I reached out to grab her shoulder, "Don't touch me Austin," she replied to me with fear written all over her face. She had become scared of me for the first time; I was a monster to her. She walked out of the gym and my soul began crying. While trying to keep it together on the surface, on the inside my whole world just came crumbling down. The one person I could talk to about these sorts of problems has just walked out of my life. There was nothing else left to lose.

The EMT Paramedics arrived, placing GP on a stretcher and getting him ready for transport to the nearby Doctor's Hospital for examination. I walked over to the stretcher to get a look at my friend and teammate as he lay unconscious , reminding me of the wrong I had done in this gym today. The team accompanied the paramedics taking GP to the ambulance, all showing me their disgust as they brushed by me on their way outside.

A hand shoved my shoulder, "Austin I

need you in the press conference with Jim in 5 minutes, lower level lobby, " Dino said to me. Coach Dino was always really good about dealing with the press which is why they always respected his wishes. He knew to call a press conference announcing the brawl before major news media outlets began telling the story themselves. He wanted Coach Donahue to deliver the facts before stories began being fabricated and he wanted me by his side. I didn't want to go. It was my fault that all of this happened and I didn't want to do anything but quit the team.

Time passed and the gym cleared as we made our way to the press room down stairs in the lobby. "I'm disappointed in you Austin, just know that," Coach

Donahue said to me. There was no excuse for my behavior so the only response I could muster up was, "I apologize." The lights began to brighten up in the press room signifying the beginning of the press conference:

Coach Donahue delivered the speech:

"Thank you for coming; we need not waste time. Our players were participating in a very intense practice before emotions ran rampant causing a small fight to break out between our junior guard, Austin Arrington and Freshman, Armonti Perry. Punches were thrown and things escalated quickly causing injuries to both Armonti Perry and Gerard Penny. Penny has been taken to Doctor's Hospital for further

examination. Suspensions have not been handed out from the front office but once we get things sorted out we will let the media know but as of right now, no suspensions have been handed down in the locker room."

Coach's pause caused for a stir in the pressroom as press officials began fighting for positions to ask questions. Dino directed the impromptu press conference, "Ladies and gentleman would you all calm down, please take your seats." The room got quiet as Dino continued, "I'll be directing the press conference from here on out, any questions please raise your hand… Have to treat you all like 5th graders." Hands reached for the sky quickly, Dino surveyed the room before calling on an overweight white man claiming to be from ESPN Radio, "YOU," Dino said to the man, "Introduce yourself and then ask your question."

"Mark Plummer, ESPN….. There were all types of reports claiming that the fight was started by Austin, is that true? What happened?" said the reporter.

I immediately began sweating because I knew that I had started the fight and I didn't want to become the enemy of state. I think coach could look at the anguish on my face as he quickly said, "That question is inappropriate, more details will be released at a later date."

Frustrated, Plummer continued, "Oh come

on, he's right there. Look kid [talking to me], did you start the fight or not?"

Dino began walking over to Mr. Plummer and the Press Room began to murmur. "Ok buddy you have to go and you are no longer allowed on these premises, I don't care who cuts your checks," Dino said to Plummer. As Plummer began reaching for his jacket, my first taste of true manhood began to kick in as I suddenly felt the most guilt I have ever felt throughout this entire situation. All of a sudden I wanted to speak up and answer the question, taking the blame for the entire situation.

"Yes, it was my fault," I mumbled into the Press Room microphone. The room froze as they were shocked that I responded and took the blame for the entire ordeal.

The reporters began grabbing their recorders as the lights seemed to get brighter. "What happened?" Plummer calmly asked. The entire country was waiting for this answer and I knew that this moment would be remembered in University of Maryland history. It was the moment I really fell in love with Media and Communications because it was at this moment I realized the power it embodies. I was going to be as honest as possible with hopes of helping someone else become a better leader than I was. I wanted the world to know that I know I made a mistake and wanted fix things. I wanted people to see the importance of fixing their mistakes.

"To be honest with you Mark, I have been

a horrible leader. I was having a bad practice – A bad few months honestly you know, trying to deal with the cut in my playing time. Things had become a lot." The camera flashes were so loud; the lights were so bright. I couldn't turn back. "I made a bad move of trying to embarrass my younger teammate in efforts of getting my starting position back and everything exploded like I knew it would. I knew I could get him to his boiling point and I shouldn't have. I- I -....
–It was just bad leadership.... Poor choice of judgment and I apologize. I apologize to the fans for having to deal with this, I mean.... Who knows what trouble I may have just caused. I apologize for embarrassing my coach; allowing my anger to get the best of me. I apologize to

my team mates and fellow Terrapins for letting us down and causing this kind of trouble and... I'm just sorry. I didn't think things would turn out like this....."

The pressroom was silent as I think most of them were shocked to hear such a young man speak about his downfalls so fluently. I THINK THEY FELT THE PASSION AND SINCERITY WITHIN MY APOLOGY AND IT GAVE EVERYONE GOOSE BUMPS. I tried to hold back the tears but I gave up as the first tear fell down the left side of my face. I dropped my head in defeat, my heart pounding. My throat felt swollen and my soul felt cold.

"Austin, Denise Blane from the Washington Post, what have you learned from this?" a question bellowed from the lights.

I wiped my eyes, gathered my emotions and responded, " I've learned what true leadership is. I learned, you know…. How important it is. It's so many ways to handle situations and often times we don't think of the repercussions of our childish decisions. I'm just sorry…. I don't know if I'm still a member of this team or what will come of this but I didn't mean for all of this to happen."

My entire body broke out into a cold sweat, I really didn't know what was happening. I kind of just wanted to get up from this panel, go to the locker room, change clothes and go for a run.

"That was very leader-like of you to take the heat for this, your story isn't over Austin, thank you for answering my question," Denise continued. Little did she know this is exactly what I needed to hear; Somebody recognized my desire to lead successfully. That's all I wanted.

A slight pause in the press conference made room for the press members to begin shouting more questions before Coach Dino stepped in.

Coach Dino dismissed the Press Conference and I walked out with Coach Donahue's arm around my neck. Although the guilt still lingered, I felt relieved in knowing that I had been completely honest about the entire situation and was willing and ready to deal with the repercussions.

"We'll make sure you come back from this Austin, I'm glad you are growing with us," Coach Donahue said to me.

After this long day, I just wanted to either go home or go see my lady. I wondered if she was still mad at me about what took place at practice earlier? Is she still scared of me? I needed her now more than ever and without her I can't bounce back from this situation. I finally made it back to the locker room and I didn't even shower. My phone was ringing off the hook and I answered for no one, not even my mother. I knew everyone wanted to just be nosy or try and put me down and I didn't want anything to do with it. I finally slid my Levi jeans on, my Maryland Basketball hoodie and laced up my Timberland boots before bracing the wind of the night on a long walk back home. I grabbed my headphones and blasted Kendrick Lamar, feeling free from guilt as I laid it all out in the press conference.

I walked out of the athletic center and to my surprise, I saw Deja waiting for me on a bench directly adjacent to the back entrance of the building. Shivering and bundled up, she looked up at me with a sad and somber face. I felt the emotion all throughout her body even from 20 feet away. Our connection had grown so strong in the past 10 months that we knew how to come to each other's aid even without saying a word. I dropped my Under Armor gym bag, took off my headphones and walked to my Queen. I tried to hold it in but every emotion just whisked me away as I cried in her arms.

Sobbing I said, "How did this happen baby? I didn't want this to happen. I just wanted my spot back that's all I wanted." I don't know how she could understand anything I was saying because I was sobbing so hard but before I knew it, she was crying too. There we stood in front the athletic center, holding each other crying. "How can I bounce back from this? Baby… I quit, I'm done… I'm just going to focus on us and school and just…." She pushed me away and gave me a stern look. She said, "No Austin, You will not quit."

The tone in her voice forced me to heed her request or at least listen to what she was saying, "You will not quit on this team, you will not quit on yourself and you will not quit on me. I have seen you at your best; I have seen you at your worst. I know what you are capable of and I'm not even talking about basketball skill. You have the potential to lead this team Austin, you can't bitch up and quit right now. Just because you hit a road block…. You know… Just because….. You made a mistake, that doesn't mean it's over Austin. We are going to get through this I promise."

I stood there frozen; weak. I was 6'1 on a good day but I quickly shrunk to 4'11 as I laid in her arms. I felt every word she said to me; We were going to get through this together.

We locked eyes as she reached up to wipe the tears from my face saying, "Austin, please don't let me down. Let's get through this. I believe in you baby and once we get back on the court, we are going to be better than ever and you will get a ring."

I felt defeated earlier; I felt like everything was over for me. I thought I had to find another path in life and I figured my hoop dreams were over after I caused the biggest brawl in Terrapin history. I felt like my entire world was collapsing and there was nothing that I could do about it. I felt like the end was near but now, I feel alive.

DEJA SPOKE LIFE INTO MY DEAD SITUATION AND ME. SHE HELPED ME REALIZE THAT THE SUN IS STILL SHINING AND THAT THERE IS STILL HOPE IN TOMORROW FOR ME.

She made me feel better about myself than I have felt in prior years and she helped me see that with every downfall comes the opportunity to rise again. She helped me see that my story was not over.

We walked to her dorm at Oakland Hall,

Lord Brian James

ordered some food and cut off our phones. I knew that by now the story of the brawl had probably taken over national media so we turned to ESPN to get the latest. Scrolling across the bottom of the screen read:

The NCAA Men's Basketball Organization has issued sanctions for the 4 University of Maryland players involved in Wednesday's practice brawl. Austin Arrington, Gerard Penny, Armonti Perry and Darius Pittman have all been suspended 4 games a piece.

I think Deja looked at my face and could tell that the news hurt me. She said, "And after those 4 games you are going to come back stronger than ever. I wish they knew what they had coming for them, this is our year baby." My confidence was boosted and I knew that this was our year too. I was going to lead this team; my lady helped me realize that.

She spoke life into me and brought me to my full potential.

I looked over at her with a piercing look of love and passion. I could hear her heart beat as you could penetrate the sexual tension in the room with a butter knife. My hand slid up her thigh as I leaned in for a kiss, pinning her down on the black leather couch.

It was a night I will never forget; the first night we made love.

Chapter IV
Soil Of Love
4 The Passion Has Been Liquified

This chapter is dedicated to Indianapolis, a city who was nice enough to stand at the end of the dark tunnel, swinging a dim lamp.

December 17th, 2020

SHE BEGAN TO tremble as my hands began to explore her smooth terrain; her comfort hadn't been violated like this before. This was our first time and she had never done this before. The goose bumps on her neck began to wave at me, signaling a green light to continue. Her eyes were closed and she was lost in the moment. We were in love; to call this lust would be disrespectful. I've slept with a lot of women but I've never made love. I must admit, I was nervous too.

About a month after we started dating, we fell victim to a hot and steamy night in my parents' home. She was visiting me and needless to mention, we missed each other. The energy of absence created a sexually hostile environment that ended with us basically naked on my mother's tan cloth couch. She stopped me before I could pull down her panties and I knew what she was signaling.

Things calmed down and we started to talk and that's when she revealed to me that she was a virgin. She told me that she had gotten close to losing her purity in her freshman year but since then, she had been with no one. She told me that she didn't know when she would be ready but she assured me that one day our emotions will rise so high that we wouldn't be able to stop ourselves and then on that day, we would make love.

-This was that.

As she pulled my soul closer with her tongue, I could feel the energy and emotion being transferred as we exchange body heat on this cold December night. I could feel all of her worries and painful emotions being let go and surely she could feel the stress in my world diminishing. I had been with many women before but I had never made love.

-This was that.

She started to unzip my Maryland Basketball sweatshirt as her nipples began to protrude through her Maryland Basketball shirt. As we continued to kiss intensely, I began to lift up her shirt, exposing her beautiful bronze skin to the hot and sexually charged air that had filled the room. I knocked over my Terrapin blanket trying to position myself in reference to her unbelievable body.

She pushed me away slightly, not aggressively, as she proceeded to remove her own shirt all the way. I stared into her beautiful, captivating eyes as she removed her bra, exposing her breasts. As I was staring into her eyes, I gazed down at her upper body in complete awe of the perfection that God had created with this woman. I locked eyes with her once more as I completely removed my sweatshirt. She then pulled on my undershirt to help me remove it faster, showing me that it was time.

I had slept with many women but I had never made love before. This was that.

Never did I ever feel so weak but in charge. Never have I ever felt so thankful to God for creating someone like this woman who is sitting in front of me half-naked. Never have I ever thanked God for a woman before in my life (Who wasn't my mother). She began to reveal a slight grin as we sat there staring at each other before she put her arms around my neck.

She stared into my eyes, "I love you

Austin."

MY HEART NEARLY POUNDED OUT OF MY CHEST AS THOSE WORDS WENT INTO MY EARS AND THEN INTO MY SOUL, PURIFYING THE DIRTY WATERS OF MY PAST AND CLEANSING MY SPIRIT.

"I love you too, baby," I replied to her. Words that felt so real to me like never before.

This was that.

She pulled me closer to her and we began to kiss again as she began to run her hands up and down my arms, exposing her self to the stories on my skin. She always loved my tattoos; I could feel that now. I pinned her down on the couch once more as we continued to violently kiss.

Unlocking lips, a strand of saliva still connected our mouths as I slowly began to pull away about 4 inches from her face. I looked into her eyes before targeting my next location, dragging my tongue across her jugular vein until she started to moan. I slightly bit her neck as she dug her fingernails in my bare-back. She dragged her fingers about 2 inches across my back, scratching marks into my Teres Major area.

My hands, bored on the arm of the couch, began to caress her stomach, tickling her belly ring. Kissing her neck and roaming her abdomen area, she couldn't take it- this is where she wanted to be. I slid my hands up to gently caress her 34C breasts, as I then began to massage them. I slid my tongue down from her jugular in search of her perky nipple, traveling about 6 ½ inches down her neck and a few inches to the right. I began to lick around her breasts as she continued to moan uncontrollably.

The connection was surreal as we began breathing together, our heartbeats synchronized and we were moving as one.

-This was that.

Her hands began to travel, grabbing my penis with force signaling that it was time.

Our love and passion had brought us here, our worlds had collided and it was time to build another; Together.

I began to unbutton and then unzip her nearly skin tight jeans, sliding them off revealing the legs of a stallion. She had one huge tattoo on her left thigh of an elephant that rested perfectly on her well-shaped and toned lower body. I slid my pants off discretely and finally removed my University of Maryland skullcap, as we lay completely naked on my leather couch. I began pushing the buttons in her garden, trying to cause a stir in her ocean. As I began to stir the wind a little faster, her facial expression reveals that the waves were rising in her world. She began to breathe even more violently as her quiet moans began to turn into grunts.

I removed my hand from her garden as I noticed the soil was moist enough to grow the roses of her soul. I looked at her, noticing the dysfunction of her hair and sweat glistening off of her forehead. She panted for breath, trying to get a grip on where she was, trying to control the waves in her soul but she couldn't; I knew just the medicine.

I leaned down and began to violently kiss her garden, turning her world upside down and she moaned uncontrollably. What was day in her world is now night and whatever darkness haunted her were now well lit crevices. Completely lost in her own ocean, she didn't know what to do with her hands as they went from nearly choking the back of my neck to damn near digging holes into my leather couch.

Our worlds had collided and it was time to build another, together. This was that.

I removed my tongue from her garden as I noticed that the soil was moist enough to grow the roses of her soul. She began to touch her own roses, in disbelief of the condition of her garden. I didn't really carry condoms but I had to rummage through my things because I had to protect her, not myself. As far I knew, I was clean. We get tested in the beginning of each season as a part of our physicals and nothing had come up in the results but I loved this girl so much, I didn't want to hurt her just in case.

But, to no avail.

"Austin," she moaned to me as she continued to rub the roses.

"I can't find a rubber, " I said to her.

I don't know whether it was the serotonin talking but she replied, "I trust you baby, just get over here."

When you're in a strong and thriving relationship, the "need" to carry condoms diminishes, especially if you are with a virgin. I never carried them and honestly that was a good thing. That means that I never even expected to put myself in situations where I would need a condom. I truly loved this girl and only this girl.

I climbed back on top of her, strong and erect, we braced ourselves for impact. I would be lying if I said that she was the only one nervous; I had never been in this situation before. All of the other girls that I have been with had no emotional attachment at all, the deed was easy to get done. This felt like the most real sexual encounter I had come across in my life.

Her hands slid down my lower back and my hands held my 6 foot, 182 pound frame up over her body. She used her fingers to pull my body towards hers, inviting my wand into her garden. Slowly, we accepted the invitation as I began to churn the waves of her world once more. Stroke after stroke, I began to harp on why it never worked with other women in the past. As we began making true and genuine love, I began to understand every single thing that ever went wrong with my past relationships, it all made sense now.

She screamed abruptly, digging her nails into my back once more. Stroke after stroke, she moaned as I kept entering and exiting her garden. Remnants of her soil began to leak down the leather couch as I grabbed her legs and placed them over my shoulders. With power, grace, love and passion I began to penetrate her garden once more, thrusting away all of the fear and pain that haunted us individually. Our souls became friends that day agreeing to heal every bit of pain within our lives; Agreeing to become one.

We sped up as we both were near detonation.

There we were, two lovers breathing on one accord without a care in the world. I completely ignored every bad thing they were saying about me in the background on ESPN. Actually, I completely forgot that I might have just had the roughest day of my little life. None of that mattered now as we were a few thrusts away from detonation.

"AUSTIN!" she screamed.

"Hold on baby," I moaned back to her as I continued to stir her garden trying to fulfill my mission.

"AUSTIN!" she screamed again as the

remnants of her soil began leaking down the black leather couch again. I moaned (really loud this time). I unplugged her garden with haste due to fear of mixing soil and seed, and detonated onto the ground. We took some time to catch our breaths as we both just experienced a life-changing feat, barely being able to breathe at this point.

Weak but pleased, I rolled her over to switch positions so that she was resting her body on mine. I squeezed her tightly, holding her close enough to feel each other's heartbeats. We were one. I then grabbed the Terrapin blanket that had fallen onto the floor and covered us with it. SKIN ON SKIN, SOUL ON SOUL, WE WERE ONE. SHE FELL

ASLEEP IN MY ARMS.

That was that.

It was safe to say that she created the best year of my life that school year. Things just began to change for me after that night. Our bond was nearly unbreakable at this point; we had thrown away our single identities and lived as one from that point on.

The next morning I began a regiment that changed my life as I began to get up every morning at 5 and go into the gym to shoot around. I believed every word that Deja said to me that night, "After your 4 game suspension, you're going to be unstoppable." She made me believe in myself and she gave me the energy to get up and be great. She believed in me and I knew it after that night. She watched me become a leader that year.

We had practice that next evening and although we were suspended, we still had to practice with the team. The only changes were that we were all running on the secondary squad to prepare the team to be without us for the next 4 games. I had found my niche as a sort of silent assassin on the team, not really saying much just being more of a hermit crab. I knew that GP was the talkative (sometimes verbally abusive) one so I figured his leadership skills was all the team needed. Things changed though. After that December 10th night, after witnessing the strength and power of true love I became alive.

"Fellas, you all can do this without us. We made a mistake and now we have to pay for it but y'all will carry the torch, I believe in you! " I said to my team as we were just getting ready to begin the intra-squad scrimmage. "Feeling like a leader today huh, Aust?" Coach said to me. I chuckled a little bit and yelled to the rest of the team, "Aight fellas, let's go!"

As the scrimmage started I was a new man. I began teaching the younger players as opposed to trying to embarrass them. I began trying to empower the players who would have to lead our team to victory over one of the toughest teams in the nation, Texas Longhorns. I was giving pep talks to players and I was vocal about getting our Terrapin team to play at it's absolute highest potential. I was a different animal.

The scrimmage concluded, and game day was in two days. The team was leaving first thing in the morning and this would probably be my last time seeing them before they left since we weren't allowed to travel with the team during suspension. I knew I had become a man:

"Fellas, I just want you all to know that I love y'all man. I know yesterday was a tough day in the history of our team; a bad day for us man.... Niggas was really fighting though," I said as everyone began to chuckle. I continued, "But seriously, man

what happened yesterday goes to show you the passion that we have as a team. We came close last year to winning it all and this year is our year. We want it bad enough.... That's all it was yesterday baby, that.... That.... That energy of wanting to succeed, it just got the best of us... Now we have to channel that energy and whoop ass against Texas. [Dramatic pause] Listen man, I'm sorry for the drama and trouble that I caused man.... I let this team down because I couldn't handle the heat, I apologize fellas...."

"It's aight boy," the team began to reply.

"Naw, listen I got to do better... And I will do better.... Don't worry about me, y'all go kick some Longhorn ass and we'll be here when you get back. This is our year fellas! TERPS ON 3.... 1....2....3 !" I said to my team, they replied with an energetic and jublilant, "TERPS!"

Coach Donahue, who is known for his corny responses interjected, "Yeah, what he said!" The team laughed as we broke huddle and the gym was filled with positive energy and laughter as our practice concluded in a much more peaceful manor than 24 hours prior. I looked across the gym at the Terps staff having a small meeting and I locked eyes with the love of my life, Deja. While trying to also be attentive to her boss who was prepping his team for the trip to Texas, she winked at me and let off a grin to show her approval of me. I loved her.

Smiling, I looked away and saw Darius Pittman and Amonti Perry across the gym, sitting on the bleachers looking down. I knew what the two young players were thinking, I knew the regret they were feeling while watching their team mates prepare for possibly the biggest game of our season. I walked over to the two young men and addressed them as such:

"Fellas, keep your head up man. We gonna be aight."

I could tell that Amonti was still a little disgusted with me and my antics the day before, "Yo, AP you one hell of a player man. Both of you are. I wish I had half of the talent that y'all have for real…. Man….

I'm sorry about yesterday for real. I mean…. we are better than that. We're teammates and that's what we are going to be." I continued to them. I reached out my hand in a bit of a truce, attempting a handshake and after a slight pause Amonti smiled and accepted my handshake. Laughing he said, "Yeah, I bet you want no part of big boy over here [pointing to Darius]." I also shook hands with Darius who was laughing as well.

GP had been taken to the hospital and discharged over night but I knew that it would make things even better if I could convince my two young players to come with me to visit him in his room, "Y'all know GP is back in his room right now," I said to them. "I want y'all to go get dressed and then let's go visit him."

The boys agreed and we took GP some Pizza Hut that night, laughing and talking about basketball. We even broke out NBA 2K and played a few rounds of that before we left and went our separate ways. My lady had to fly out with the team in the morning so I knew she would be in my arms tonight. She met me at my house and we made love again; passion filled the air.

"I'm proud of you," she said. She then pointed to my chest, "Now we get to see what's really inside of there."

I had been with a lot of women but never made love before. I never felt the power of love ever in my life but now it was an undeniable feeling that proved it's power as I lay next to this woman as a completely different man that the night before. She fell asleep in my arms once more.

We lost to the No.7 Texas Longhorns. It was a game closer than many expected but without Darius, Amonti, Gerard and myself, we didn't have enough gas in the tank to run with such a strong team.

That game was just the beginning to the second best season in Terrapin history.

IT WAS THE BEGINNING OF ONE OF THE MOST SUCCESSFUL CHAPTER OF MY LIFE AND I OWE IT ALL TO HER. I OWE IT ALL

TO DEJA.

She created the best year for me by speaking life into my future. She knew that this year was on the horizon.

Chapter V

An Enriching Love

5 An Angel's Mission.

This chapter is dedicated to Indianapolis, a city who was nice enough to stand at the end of the dark tunnel, swinging a dim lamp.

Monday April 4th, 2021

COMING OUT OF a timeout, walking past the scorers' table, I overheard the commentators:

"What a season this has been for this underrated University of Maryland team; a Season that began with much controversy

with the uh.... Brawl at College Park... the 4 game suspensions. Emotions running high at the beginning of the season. They started off the season down four men John, 4 of their most important pieces... Went 2-2 on the beginning of the season and now here they are, NCAA National Championship.... 47 seconds remaining in the game, tie game- Terps battled back from a 13 point deficit to the Wildcats....What a game from Maryland's star, Gerard Penny & fantastic showing from their Junior Point Guard, Austin Arrington.... 18 points 16 assists... Just phenomenal... this is a historical-"

The horn blew and I shifted my focus to what was happening on the court. My entire life's work to this point had been in preparation for this moment. Every single little league game foreshadowed this moment and here I am; In the national spotlight. The entire world watched us climb from one of the darkest moments in Terrapin history, to one of the most coveted stages in College Basketball. The world saw me at my worst; to be honest, much of the world met me at my worst but that was the past. I am a man now.

I had come a long way since that fight at practice. My vocal tone changed and I operated in the trenches of life with a northeastern sense of stoicism, simply focused on accomplishing a goal. Our team had gelled together and been dubbed the nickname, 'the Dirty Dozen' as we had proven all year long that any of our 12 players could dominate the court. We were counted out in the beginning after the brawl but we fought through the turbulent times and ended the season as the No. 2 rated team in the nation behind the No.1 Kentucky Wildcats. Although we were No. 2 in the national ranking, we were a top seed in the National tournament and the underdog in the championship battle. Although most of the press thought that Kentucky would rip us apart, we were a fan favorite as America fell in love with our story of resiliency.

This game had been a true dogfight from the beginning – For us at least. They knew all of our weaknesses and they accentuated them on each of us, one by one. They knew first of all that although I had built a strong and confident tone as a leader, I still was not as confident on the big stages and had a fear of driving the lane with my left hand. No matter how strong I had gotten over the past few months, both mentally and physically, I still was not ready to terrorize the paint. As a matter of fact, much of my stats came from my nearly perfect 3-point percentage and my innate ability to always hone in on whoever had the hot hand on offense. They pressed me up and down the court, creating a sense of discomfort for me most of the game until towards the end, where we were able to capitalize on their fatigue.

GP had matured a lot as well but

Kentucky was out to take him back to his prior self, purposefully trying to ignite his anger on every play. At the end of each possession they would bump, fight, and shove GP, mumbling snarky, and sardonic remarks at the nation's top player. After one play in the beginning of the second half, Kentucky's Freshman Power Forward, Jackson Bailey III, shoved GP and after playing nearly an hour of a heated battle, GP exploded. He charged toward Bailey with rage in his eyes and our entire team was fearful of what would happen next:

"Aye man, you got to do all that extra bullshit because you ain't got no game bitch. Push me again and I'll bust your fuc-," he said to Bailey before we ran over to break up the argument. The refs had been blowing their whistles as they were trying to keep a clean game, charging both GP and Jackson Bailey with a technical foul. Coach had to sit GP down to cool him off but Kentucky was celebrating because they accomplished their mission to get our star player out of the game, figuratively and literally.

They also knew and took advantage of Darius' youth under the basket. Darius (Pittman) was a big body in the paint but he didn't know his strength just yet. Although age is simply a number, he fell victim to deference. He had the fight in him and could play with the best in college basketball but he would have to play his absolute best; No mistakes. He was equivalent to a super hero who didn't know his own strength. All season we had been preparing him for this moment trying to help him become more confident in his implausible abilities but, every ounce of progress we had made with him had been wiped clean in the first period of the National Championship. They shut us down.

We fought our way back from a 13-point halftime deficit; A game that felt like we were down 26 points. I specifically remembered looking over into the third row of the stands during a timeout in the second half, making eye contact with my beautiful mother (Rest her soul) as she smiled at me and mouthed the words, "I

Love you!" I THINK SHE COULD SEE THAT WE WERE MENTALLY DRAINED AND THAT ALTHOUGH I WAS HAVING THE BEST SEASON OF MY LIFE, THIS BATTLE WAS GETTING THE BEST OF ME. I felt the love from my mother, an energy that I knew all too well as she was always there for me. I then looked a few chairs over to find Deja in her Maryland basketball gear, with her hands clutched over her mouth, nearly as anxious as I was. She had been extremely successful in her career endeavors over the past few months and was actually covering the game for her class. Her anguish quickly transformed to a giggle as she pointed to me and mouthed, "You got this!"

I WAS ALWAYS A FIRM ADVOCATE THAT NOTHING IS STRONGER THAN THE ENERGY OF TRUE LOVE AND I HAD BEEN REASSURED OF THAT IDEOLOGY THAT NIGHT. We broke the huddle that timeout and I knew that I had to recharge our team and get us back in this game. Minute by minute, I led the team's comeback over this 20 minute period and whether it was an assist or basket, I was involved on every play up until this point. I knew that our only way to get a victory in this game was for me to take the helm and drive our team to a historical and monumental championship. You see, they had figured out that GP was our weapon I mean, the entire country knew that. They had so much emphasis on him that on almost every play, I was left nearly wide open and free to do what I wanted. I knew that in order for us to be victorious, I would have to capitalize on their poor defensive strategy.

The whistle blew and the play was live. The ball was passed in to me and the clock began to roll as I looked up at the jumbo-tron in the huge, illustrious Lucas Oil Stadium. I battled against a weak and tired "Full Court Press" as I brought the ball up the court. Coach wanted to strike fast and efficient, taking advantage of their ignorance on defense. I got to the top of the key, located GP who was coming off of a screen, and handed the ball off to him. The Wildcats quickly shifted their defense to double team against GP and I was able to get open near the right baseline corner. "G! You got help! You got help!" I yelled as the Wildcats quickly noticed their defense breaking down. The clock continued to roll as GP found me and passed me the ball in the corner. Just then, the Freshman Wildcat Center, Devin Whitaker was guarding Darius Pittman and quickly left Darius to try and meet me in the corner to prevent an open shot. I noticed the break down in the defense and did a quick touch pass to Darius where he was nearly wide open for the lay up. The Wildcat defenders panicked and swarmed Darius as he went up for the lay up before they intentionally fouled him.

"Shooting foul, Number 24, Michael McDougle… that's his 3rd personal foul, 6th team foul…. At the line shooting 2 for the Terrapins, Darius Pittman," said the announcer.

Now, usually this would excite me because of the easy points that would put us ahead with 32 seconds left on the clock but I was actually worried this time. Darius was a less than exceptional free throw shooter and actually was 2/8 tonight from the free throw line. Kentucky called yet another time out to try and rattle our young freshman big man and I have to say it may have sufficed as an anxiety booster. Pittman returned from the timeout and missed both of the free throws.

Kentucky got the rebound after the miss and came up court with the opposite intentions as our possession prior. They tried to drain the clock down to zero, passing the ball around the top of the key as the seconds wind down on the clock. I had 3 fouls to give so I intentionally fouled one of the Wildcat guards. We were in the penalties so my foul would send their Sophomore Shooting Guard, DeMarcus Jones to the line for a 1-and-1 shot.

"This over bro. Y'all had a good run but it stops here homie," Jones said to me as he prepared to shoot his shots. "1 and 1!" the ref yelled to DeMarcus as he passed him the ball at the free throw line. DeMarcus shot and made his first free throw but the second rimmed out. Darius made the play of the season by grabbing the game saving rebound and GP called a timeout the minute Darius cleaned the boards.

The stoppage in play put us at half-court for the beginning of the next possession and something told me in my soul that what would happen next would be a life changing event. I had always been super spiritual as a person and believed in signs but I never heard God's voice as loud as I heard him that night. I looked up at the jumbo-tron before we put the ball in play and I saw with my own eyes, myself making the game winning shot. It felt so real that it gave me the confidence I needed to flourish on this play. I knew we were going to win this game.

With 7 seconds left on the clock, the whistle blew and I used my most evasive tactics to get just enough space to get the inbound pass. I watched the clock tick down and I could see the fear on this young Kentucky squad's face. They weren't scared of me though they were scared of GP. They should have been scared of me and what I'm capable of but I was surely ready to convince them. They chose not to double-team me at the top of the key, which would be a decision that they would never forgive themselves for.

I took on DeMarcus and his youth showed as he gave me about 7 inches of space to take a shot with a 1 second left on the clock. I didn't even watch it go in. I automatically knew what was bound to happen. The shot went in and the stands erupted in pandemonium. I immediately fell to the floor and cried my heart out. My team began to pile on top of me as the confetti fell from the sky and the crowd cheered for what seemed like forever. I couldn't even enjoy this moment because I couldn't stop crying. I never picked my head up to look up at the lights; I never looked at any of the fans' faces. I honestly lost myself in that moment.

My team picked me up as I covered my face to conceal my emotions. They dragged me from right inside of the 3-point line and carried me to middle of the court where our fans and families were celebrating. I felt miserable because I hid my face from the fans that held us down this entire season but there were so many emotions running through my body at that point.

The salient emotion was that I was a true witness to the power of love and in that split second it felt almost as if God strategically placed Deja in my life. She revived my dying passion for my God given talent, transforming me from a failing Junior Point Guard to a National Champion. She encouraged me at the beginning of that year to become abreast with what God had planned for me and not to give up but to simply grow up. There was power in that four-letter word that lined itself with her actions and energy, a power that turned me into a champion; A power that turned me into a man.

Reporters swarmed me at half-court and although I was too choked up to really give a great interview, I said one line that told the world how I really felt:

"Love man... True love man, there is power in true love. God... Family... My lady... Friends.... True love will do it," I responded to a reporter who asked about my "secret power" that propelled me through this season.

We popped champagne in the locker room and went out to celebrate at

Terrapin Turf the next night after we returned back to College Park but, the best part of the night was to come. Deja had been quiet about her accomplishments since I was trying to focus on getting us through the National Tournament. She didn't reveal to me the good news that she had received an offer to do the coveted active internship at one of the local stations, NBC 4. Her best friend, Essence, had revealed the amazing news to me and I couldn't contain myself. Students in her program were fighting to get that internship because of the great benefits. Students in the program were paid and also got the opportunity to make appearances on air and they were almost guaranteed a job offer upon graduation.

We had been so busy in the tournament that she never had the chance to break the news to me and I had been absent during her application process. Now that I knew about the internship, we had to celebrate.

I was always the guy who brought his girlfriend to the club and honestly, I didn't care about it. Having her at the club with me actually helped me to have fun and my night didn't really become fun until she walked into Terrapin Turf. We were in a booth area sitting around a restaurant style table when she and her friends walked in, close to 1 am.

I had turned my head to talk to one of our teammates when I felt a body come sit on my lap and say, "Somebody sitting here?"

I had no clue who it was at first so I kind of shoved this person before I realized that it was the love of my life, the woman to whom I really owed all of this celebration.

"Don't be sneaking up on me like that girl," I said in her ear as I started to lightly tickle her side until she giggled and squirmed. I was up to something and she had absolutely no clue.

The team was in on it too, GP looked at me and Deja across the table and said over the music, "Austin, let's go get some food man. IHOP sounds like the move."

"Sounds like the move to me too, let's go," I replied to him. Deja looked confused because she had just gotten to the party with her friends and was expecting to kick it with us. "Baby, I Just got here," she said to me. I smiled at her (lightly) and told her that I didn't want to be here anymore and that she and her friends had to come with us. After a little kick back, she obliged my request and she and her friends followed us to the door.

I was a sucker for surprising people and I almost gave it away. I just couldn't wait to see her glow.

She didn't know that I had found out about her internship acceptance and she also didn't know that I had planned this surprise party while we were playing the Final Four in Indianapolis. While in Indianapolis for the tournament, I had told coach about how I felt bad about not being there for Deja while she was applying for her internship. He knew a lot about our relationship considering the fact that I played for him and she (essentially) worked for him. He was a big fan of our companionship simply because much like the rest of the world, he was a witness to what she had done for my life.

"Coach, what am I supposed to do?" I asked him. He assured me that because he was my coach and somewhat of a road father, he would give me and the team a celebration at the IHOP in College Park. We were big fans of IHOP; it was our post practice spot every year since I have been a Terp. Coach had paid to have the IHOP shut down for just players and close friends but assured me that we would celebrate Deja's success as well that night. Almost like, the celebration was really for her and masked as a team event.

We had gone to IHOP a couple of hours earlier and decorated the entire eatery with all types of celebratory décor. Walking into the restaurant, there was a row of balloons in Red and Black along with a small red carpet once you enter the actual dining area. There was a huge "Congrats Deja" sign over the main eating area. She loved Colorado omelets and we made sure her table was set. There was a cake with my face on it, giving the 'thumbs up' sign, which read 'Congrats Baby!' IHOP broke the rules for us allowing us to bring in bottles of Champagne for her and the rest of the team to have with our breakfast (at night?). The plan was simple: Bring Deja in, take her straight to her table, Say a few words about her, and then let Coach take over the rest of the party.

Show time.

I made a pit stop at 7-11 before arriving at IHOP so that we could get there after the rest of the team. Her friends were in on this too; they hopped in the other cars with my teammates, leaving Deja and me alone. We arrived at the IHOP and she immediately made a comment about how empty the eatery was which was unusual at this time of night. I escorted her into the restaurant where she started to notice the decorations and then pointed out that this was a party to celebrate the team, "Oh you guys rented out the place huh? All it took was one championship huh?" she said to me in a snarky tone.

The minute we walked into the main dining area, the team yelled, "Surprise!" and she was completely lost. I pulled her close and whispered in her ear, "Surprise baby! Congrats on your NBC internship! I love you so much." She broke down crying nearly uncontrollably and at that point, the entire room believed in love once again. We all circled around to congratulate her on her accomplishments and cut the cake. We then popped champagne and let Coach take over to honor our team with our friends. There I sat with my Queen on my lap, endless pancakes and a huge smile on my face.

Coach spoke:

"You know, it must be major if my old ass is out this late. [laughter from audience] No but seriously, what a great group of individuals here tonight... Well, morning rather. I have watched this team grow, I saw each of you as children and now I stand amongst men. I'm so happy for you. Not just you know... as a team but also as each of you individually. I mean, come on... A National Championship? You're the best in the country. We started off in trouble man.... And it's all Austin's fault [laughter from audience]. But... I thought we were in for a rough season you know? But I

watched you all become men... The world witnessed you become champions. That's why this is the greatest American sports story. Resiliency. You did that.... I'm proud of all of you. I'm proud of our team captains, Mr. Gerard Penny [Pause during applause] and Mr. Austin Arrington [pause for applause]. Deja, I don't know what you did but don't ever leave Austin, he owes you a ring. [laughter from the audience] a championship ring, a championship ring.... I'll move on though... Oh and congratulations to you too (To Deja), I mean you worked so hard for Terrapin Basketball, Austin wouldn't shut up about you and he planned this for you, he wanted to make sure you knew that he was proud of you and he loves you very much. We all know that..... [Back to entire room] Now fellas, I can't tell you how you guys make me feel. I love each every one of you... Let's do it all again next year! Terps, Raise your glasses [referring to a toast of champagne]. We toast to the scary, dark road that a man must travel to leave the world of youth to become a man. This is to champions."

The room erupted in applause as we started to do our Maryland basketball chant. Just as we were getting ready to dig into our endless breakfast, GP stood up and I knew what his announcement was about to be.

"Wait fellas, before we leave I have something to share with my family, I wanted you all to be the first to know," he exclaimed to the room. GP was a top recruited player coming into our basketball program as a Freshman, many saw him as a 'one and done' player but the potential of bringing a National Championship to College Park kept him returning to play as a Terrapin. Without question, he could have been a solid lottery pick as a Freshman in the draft but after these past 3 years of supreme domination in his career, he is without a doubt in the running to be the top pick in this year's draft; I knew what his announcement was going to be.

GP spoke, "Fellas, an agent contacted me and warned me that several NBA teams are looking take me with the number 1 pick in this year's draft. I believe in this team so much, I never felt like this about a team, I mean you guys are one strong group of players…. We went 12 men deep in the National Championship, no team did that before. I think this is my year to enter into the NBA draft and truly chase my dream of being in the-"

Our senior forward and class clown, Buggsy Thompkins, cut off GP and said, "My nigga! YOU GOING TO THE LEAGUE BOY! Turn up!" After Buggsy's intrusion, the room erupted in applause as we were the first ones to know that our boy GP was going to be a NBA star and probably the number 1 pick in the NBA draft. He continued, "But hold up though! Everybody wait [Pause while people re-directed their attention], I want Deja to be the first to tell the world."

Deja could not believe what GP just said, "Me?" she asked. "Yes you," he responded "You the only reporter in this room… Real one at least [Sarcastically mentioning me]." You see, in the media world, an exclusive was like winning the lottery, especially an exclusive like this. This would go on to be the beginning of a long and prosperous career for Deja who will be the first person in the world to announce that the NCAA's most electrifying player will be entering the NBA Draft.

"GP, Oh my God thank you. That … that…." Deja said to GP.

"Girl, if you don't hurry up and tweet it out so we can pop these other champagne bottles and eat pancakes," he replied to her.

We popped the cork on some champagne and enjoyed our breakfast at night. Deja never left my arms, you would have thought we were a new couple. It was arguably one of the best nights in my life thus far. That night I looked around at this huge reminder of the power of love.

WITH MY QUEEN IN MY ARMS AND MY PROBLEMS IN THE REAR-VIEW, I FELT AMAZING.

Little did I know how much I would really need her healing love in the coming months.

Chapter VI
Withering Roses of Love
6 Winning the Losing Lottery

This chapter is dedicated to Indianapolis, a city who was nice enough to stand at the end of the dark tunnel, swinging a dim lamp.

July 5, 2021

THE NEXT FEW months felt like a movie; the world was perfect for about 90 days. I had declined to forego my senior year in college and enter the draft, mainly because nothing was guaranteed with my professional career right now. Although I had a completely remarkable and unbelievable season, I still hadn't proven the consistency to grab the trust of the

NBA scouts. GP's agent talked to me a few times in passing and had mentioned that some teams were interested in giving me a shot as an undrafted free agent but I figured it wasn't worth it. So, that meant that I would spend the next few months helping my best friend get ready for his dreams to finally turn on their landing lights.

It was invigorating to be able to witness the passion bleeding through GP's skin as he completely obliterated all of the Pre-Draft workouts. After the NBA Draft Lottery in the week prior, we pretty much gathered that he would be getting drafted as the number one pick to the Dallas Mavericks and expected to be the starting Shooting Guard next season. "You sure you don't want to get in on this man? Once I'm there I can make sure they sign you bro," he would always say to me. I would decline and assure him that I would join him after I graduated next year.

The draft was in a few days and his agent wanted to surprise us with a fancy dinner (still don't know if this was legal) at Benihana's downtown. All of GP's family was there and so was the blanketing emotion of excitement. The room was completely suffocated with appreciation for GP and gratitude for making everyone believe in their dreams again. Any fool could look and see that he had worked so hard to come all of this way. He swam against the some of the most treacherous of waves provided by an ocean of social media advancements as some of the most hateful words popped up on his timeline. He also bounced back from meltdowns in the locker room and on the bench, truly cleaning up his attitude and focusing on basketball. As he smiled across the packed restaurant, I couldn't help but think about how he went out and got help for his alcoholism, quietly healing his soul from a hard future. He also continued to medically handle his bi-polar disorder and never neglected to be attentive in the classroom.

I COULD HONESTLY SAY THAT I WAS TRULY PROUD OF MY BEST FRIEND, GERARD PENNY.

He delivered a chilling speech that I will never forget:

"Listen everyone, I just wanted to say thank you. Man, I would not be here if it wasn't for y'all. This [is] my dream man. [Slight pause for emotional build up as GP starts to tear up] Since I was little man, this is all I wanted; to play basketball and then move my mother out the hood…. And now… it's going to happen. [turns to look at his mother] I love you mom. All of those nights you had to find a ride to come get me from practice, all of the sacrifices you made for me…. I understand now… I love you so much momma, thank you for still believing in me… A lot of people doubted me, especially this year but, you were always there. I love you so much…. Look around;

[pointing to family and friends gathered] you did this by yourself. I'm so thankful ma, you just don't know. [Redirecting attention to entire room] I'm thankful for everyone man, I wouldn't have this moment without you all. Ima (broken) say this and then I'll sit down and let you eat but hear me when I say that nothing is more important than real love; this right here in this room. This is what life is all about man.... I, my team, all of us man, we have been on some of the biggest stages in college sports but nothing makes me feel more alive than right now, having all of you to sit here and enjoy this meal with. I'm glad to have you in my corner and I'm thankful to have you all going forward with me.... I love all of you."

The room erupted in applause as GP took

his seat. I could honestly say that at least 12 of the 31 people present were in tears and I think it was due to the wave of emotion that surrounded GP. There was an aura around him showing that he had grown up and that he was a man standing in front of us. He had matured and the man in him finally made an appearance, relieving the child of his soul of its duties. It was magical to witness the maturation.

That night was full of love and joy as we laughed and joked over fried rice and great Japanese food. I couldn't stop staring at the love of my life, Deja, who was controlling the room with her angelic presence and warming smile. We sat at a table of 8 near the center of the room, decorated with red and black balloons and candles. GP, his girlfriend Alyssa and his mother were near the center of the table as my parents, my little brother (Devin, not Jimmy), Deja and myself filled up the chairs around them. Both my mother and GP's mother complimented Deja all night, "Deja, you are so beautiful, Goodness!"

HER RADIANT SOUL WAS ON DISPLAY, WHISPERING JOY THROUGH HER EYES WHICH KEPT EVERYONE CAPTIVATED AND KEPT ME, PROUD.

Once the night was over and the room cleared out, we all knew that the next chapter of GP's life was going to be nothing short of amazing. After all of the love that engulfed the room, we had the utmost confidence in GP's support system that we knew he was going to be a terror in the NBA. After my parents left, I decided to make a run to the little gents room (Bathroom) before walking Deja to her car and leaving myself. As I was washing my hands in the restroom, GP strolls in and we have that awkward, face-to-face conversation at the sinks of the men's room. "Aus man, I just want to say thank you dude, you are truly my boy," GP said to me. I could look on his face and tell that he was really trying not get choked up as he began to reminisce on our brotherhood and bond. "Man, you know I don't like people or the mess their drama can bring but you, man, you are really my brother. I love you dude. Thanks for getting me here," he continued.

Just that moment, I remembered the first time we met at basketball camp we were 6 years old. I remembered all of the trouble we got into over the years and all of the valleys that I didn't have to walk alone because I had a brother. I remembered the first person to tell me that we were going to win a championship. I remembered all of those nights that I wanted to quit basketball because things just weren't working out how I expected them to but he continued to pour into me and encourage me to keep fighting another day. I remembered all of the things that he had done for me as well as all of the examples of true brotherhood that I revered in his character. When the world around us was dark, we continued to see the light in each other. When that light tried to hide, we searched relentlessly until it revealed itself. What many people don't know is that we actually had the same tattoo, a piece of ink to truly commemorate the bond that we had developed over the years. The tattoo read, "Phileo" which is the Greek translation of the term, "Brotherly Love," and has been a staple to our chemistry since we got them after our sophomore season. He wasn't my best friend; He was my brother.

"I love you too man," I replied to him as I reached my hand out to do our in-game handshake that we had developed over the years. Towards the end of the shake we both started to smile, as we knew we wouldn't be doing that in the game any more as he would be moving on to bigger and better things. The odds of me getting drafted to the same team as him next year were slim to none but in a few years, I know we will doing that handshake at the All Star game together; Hopefully.

"Alright man, get out of here before they think something is up in here," he said to me jokingly as I exited the restroom. Deja was waiting patiently, talking to GP's mother near the main exit. I gave Mrs, Penny (Mama P) a hug before opening the door for my lady and heading to her car. As I opened the car door to let her in she said to me, "Want to come help me study?" She was taking classes over the summer to make for a smoother senior year and often times enjoyed my assistance with her studies. Sometimes that assistance was just in the form of a distraction and in other cases I actually helped her with her work. Didn't matter, whatever the case may be I was all in. I assured her I would head to her parent's house after I dropped off this left over food at my parent's house.

That night I helped her study a little bit but mostly was there to serve as a reliable distraction from her rigorous work load as we joked and laughed most of the night. I then "mistakenly" fell asleep at her house once her parents fell asleep, exchanging body heat with her all night. Hint: It was no mistake.

Days passed by and the big day was here; my boy was getting drafted. GP's agent, Chris Broner, thought it would be great for GP to have his family and friends on hand for the big day so he paid for us to take the train from New Carrollton station right outside of D.C, to New York for the draft. I spent that 4 hour train ride completely zoned out and excited for the big day; you would have thought I was getting drafted. GP had been there for some days as he left that night after Benihana's to go to Harlem, New York for exclusive training with a basketball guru and former Terrapin, Alonzo Price.

Our train finally arrived in the big apple at

about 2:00pm and you could feel the energy in the air once we stepped foot off of the train. New York was my favorite city that I had ever been to and anyone could look at my face and tell I was in a blissful state of mind. New York was the land of opportunity, the place where dreams were birthed and raised. The New York air hit my face and galvanized my spirit as my dreams got the jumpstart they needed.

GP met us at New York's Penn Station and we took an Uber X vehicle from the station to Junior's (Restaurant) in Brooklyn right off of Flatbush Avenue. As we were eating, a couple of fans recognized us (mostly GP) and took pictures with him as they realized that this was a photo opportunity with potentially the best player to ever play the game. GP couldn't stop smiling as he kept taking pictures with fans and soaking in the moment. Once the fandom died down and our food was served, GP said to us, "I'm nervous y'all. What if tonight doesn't go how we think it will, you know?"

I knew him and I could really hear the worry in his voice as he felt that something was a little off about tonight. Anxiously wanting to heal my brother of his worry, I began to think of all of the ways the draft could go wrong and laid them out for him with one sentence, " I'm going to be 100% honest with you, the literal worst thing that can happen is that you end up on an NBA team." I was being sarcastic in saying that it's no way possible that he wouldn't get drafted. After my statement, we continued conversation as normal and finished our meal. As expected, the owner of Junior's paid for our meal and insisted that we take a photo for their wall of celebrities and tell everyone about the cheesecake. "Hope the Knicks take you at number 3! We certainly could use you!" he said to GP as we exited the restaurant en route to the draft.

We arrived at Radio City Music Hall, which was the site for the historical night as this draft was deemed to be the "Big Draft". Sports analysts had calculated that this draft class was going to be a major asset to the NBA. At least 75% of the class was destined to make a huge impact on the league and it was also expected that GP was going to be one of the greatest players to ever play the game.

When we got into Radio City Music Hall we were directed to the green room where the top tiered players were to wait for their name to be called in the draft. We took a couple of personal pictures and posed for a few press photos but nothing could truly capture this moment and the emotion that surrounded us. I went around the room and greeted all of the players as I played against most of them at some point in my career. We were seated at the round table closest to the exit that led out onto the stage and the cameras would not stop focusing on us. A few minutes before the draft began; the NBA Network caught a quick interview with me asking about my expectations from GP:

> *Reporter: "I'm sitting here with NCAA Champion and team captain for the Maryland Terrapins, Austin Arrington, who is here supporting his former team mate and best friend, Gerard Penny in tonight's draft. Really quickly Austin, what do you expect to see from your former team mate in the NBA?"*

> *My response: " Well Adam, I knew this day was going to come along. GP is a phenomenal basketball player*

and one hell of a competitor. I think he is going to go down in history as one of the best to ever play the game.

As the interview rapped up, we got the signal that the draft was beginning and almost simultaneously, GP's phone rang. "I think I know who that is," Chris Broner said to GP as his eyes began to tear up. GP answered the call and sure enough it was the General Manager of the Dallas Mavericks, Donn Nelson who informed GP that they were in fact drafting him with the number 1 pick and will be flying him to Dallas first thing in the morning. I was so excited to see that the dream came true. The room started to notice what was going on as GP's family began to start congratulating GP. The media outlets began to report that the Dallas Mavericks have informed GP that he will in fact be the number 1 pick of the 2021 draft.

Seconds later, the draft started and NBA commissioner Adam Silver, takes the podium with his famous draft introduction, "Hello and welcome to the 2021 NBA Draft. Each year we are gifted with a new pool of talent into the NBA and each year we are blown away by the phenomenal skill that these kids introduce to the league. This year's draft is set to be a historical night and we are ready to get things started. The NBA Draft is now officially open and the Dallas Mavericks are now on the clock."

Silva exited the stage and was gone for maybe 20 seconds before he had to return with Dallas' pick. He stated, "With the first pick in the 2021 NBA draft, the Dallas Mavericks select…. Shooting Guard out of the University of Maryland, Gerard Penny." The entire music hall jumped with jubilation as GP had become somewhat of a national hero because of his persona. People had begun to take a liking to him and what he represented and on this night, the entire world was happy for him and his accomplishment.

As expected, GP dropped his head on the table in the green room trying to hide his watery eyes from the world. The wave that his dreams were surfing on had finally come crashing in and his dream became reality; he was the first pick in the 2021 NBA Draft. I walked over to pick him up out of the chair; we hugged as he wiped his face. He walked over to kiss Alyssa and then hugged Coach Donahue who was also there to support him. Finally, he went to hug his mother before resting his head on her shoulder and kissing her cheeks as she began to cry tears of joy. She then watched her boy, turned man, walk out on to the stage where the crowd broke out into an uproar of praise. GP walked to shake hands with commissioner and take pictures holding up a Dallas Mavericks jersey with his name on the back. It was official. I'll be honest with you, after GP walked off of the stage the rest of the ceremony was a blur and completely pointless.

MY BOY WAS OFFICIALLY IN THE NBA.

GP had a 10:17am flight from La Guardia to Dallas-Fort Worth Airport in the morning so, we would have to save the turn up for later. We did decide to grab some drinks downstairs at the bar in our hotel (Marriot Marquis in Manhattan) before heading back to the room. We left the Radio City Music Hall, packed into a black Mercedes G Wagon (Driving service) and had a miniature celebration/praise session as we headed back to our hotel. Mama P was in the passenger seat and was the DJ for the night, which was easily the funniest thing since Bernie Mac's 'Kings of Comedy' stand up. She would blast the radio and then turn it down to give a 'praise report' of how God blessed us by allowing GP to go to the NBA. In a strange and unexplainable way, we followed her even through her confusion. It was a good night. It felt like a dream.

We finally arrived at our hotel, I couldn't wait to get inside and call Deja and tell her all about my night at the draft and also how it inspired me to want to have an amazing season so I could join my boy in the NBA. We had that kind of love that after not talking to her for most of the day, my soul was yearning to hear her voice. The driver dropped us off at the front of the hotel; we hopped out and were on the way to the room. "You guys go ahead, I'm going to go across the street and try one of these hoagies before I get put on this NBA diet," GP said to us. Mama P reassured him that although it was across the street, it still was unsafe for him to walk over there by himself so I decided I would walk with him.

GP said to me as we were walking in, "Man, I'm so happy you're here sharing this with me man. This is the best night of my life." I could feel the gravity of his words as he truly meant every last bit of what he said. "I'm glad I'm here too. I'm proud of you man." Since the door was kind of hinged in an alleyway, we began to walk through the threshold when we heard a girl screaming down the alley way, "Help!.... Give me back my damn purse!"

We looked down the alley way to see what exactly was going on and as soon as we looked, the young lady had been pistol whipped to the ground. I IMMEDIATELY FELT A BAD ENERGY BEGIN TO SURROUND US FEELING AS IF THE GRIM REAPER WAS PLAYING AN OLD, OUT OF TUNE, PIANO IN THIS ALLEY WAY. Chills covered my body as GP yelled, "Hey, leave her alone! Give her back her purse!"

Growing up an only child and living with

his single mother, he had a fond heart for women and the protection of women. He was an advocate for domestic abuse awareness and firmly believed in the zero tolerance policy on violence against women. He also believed that it was his civic duty to protect a woman, even a stranger; sometimes to his dismay.

"Yo, man, that nigga has a gun," I said to GP but he wasn't registering with what I was saying. He backed up out of the threshold of the restaurant and began chasing the man who took this stranger's purse.

Our world can be so cold. The world we live in inhabits some of the most frigid souls and cripples our society with its insensitivity to life.

An eerie feeling began to cover my body as GP was running after this man and I began running after the GP. The grim reaper began to play his broken piano louder and louder as GP got closer to this man who was not running. The man with the gun had no fear as he began to raise his 9-millimeter glock aimed in our general direction.

"GP!" I yelled in efforts to try and get him to stop in his tracks but it was too late.

The gun fired and the slowest 3 seconds of my life began as I watched the scene unfold. The lady began to scream uncontrollably as she began gathering herself after being pistol whipped to the ground. As time moved 1 mile an hour, I watched GP fall to the ground like a character in a video game. He fell lifelessly to the ground as if he had been shot and killed instantly.

-I'll never forget it.

The shooter then fired 2 more rounds in our general vicinity, trying to hit me before aiming the gun at the screaming lady and ending her life at point blank range. The air was filled with a disgusting and deathly vitality as the pool of blood began to gather around GP's lifeless body.

The shooter hopped in a black, Honda Civic (Looked like a Civic) and sped off. "HELP! DAMN!..... HELP! SOMEBODY CALL 911!" I yelled into the night sky with hopes someone in New York could hear me. My deep toned, strong voice quickly transformed to dog like whimpers, as I could no longer talk. My throat began to feel swollen as I sit there holding my best friend in my arms; lifeless. GP had his phone out while he was running and had apparently already began to dial the emergency services as I heard, 'Hello! HELLO!' coming from the speaker of his phone.

I could not stop crying. Every ounce of my body was covered in sadness as the grim reaper continued to play his piano. My brother, my best friend, and my hero had been shot and killed in an instant. The greatest night of his life turned into the last night of his life and at this point, I really wished those last two rounds would have hit me.

Finally, I picked up his phone and gave the emergency services our location as best as I could before they notified they were already on the way as someone in the area already called them. I immediately called Alyssa and I couldn't contain myself,"Lyss! GP has been shot, we are in the alley across from the hotel.... He was just... He .... " I couldn't finish my sentence without breaking down crying and she began bellowing out in immense sadness on the other end of the phone. I kept trying to get her attention but to no avail.

 Alyssa and the rest of the family began running over as Mama P saw her only son, her hero, her pride and joy laid out lifeless in the alleyway of New York City on his draft night. She was so hurt she couldn't even cry, she just fainted off into a daze up against the alley wall. Alyssa was holding GP and I was holding Mama P; not doing the best job of staying strong. We held each other and I cried the heaviest tears in my life as they landed on her salt and pepper colored hair. The alley was filled with much sadness as people began to gather around GP, the young lady who was getting robbed, and the family. People began to notice who had just been shot and killed as the paramedics finally arrived.

Tweets began to pour in as GP was officially pronounced dead at the scene. This was officially the saddest day of my life. I had at least a little drop of hope that

GP would live but once the paramedics said he was officially deceased, the entire alley began to burst out in tears.

My heart still trembles at telling the story.

That night I lost my best friend. We didn't even know what to do at this point, we felt like it was nothing to do. We just sat in the alleyway crying and holding each other as people began walking up showing their condolences. I don't remember one word of what they said though; I was too busy trying to die to be with my brother and best friend.

We were then escorted to the hospital where they had taken GP and while sitting in the lobby, my phone rang and it was Deja. She must had heard the news. I answered the phone and tried to keep it together as best as I could but I stepped out just so I could cry to her like I really wanted to. She was the only person that could heal my soul right now and I think that she knew that.

I told her we were at the hospital trying to put the pieces together and talking to the authorities about the entire incident while also trying to dodge the media. She assured me that she would be there before sunrise and sure enough, a few hours later she walked into the emergency room at the New York Presbyterian Hospital. The minute I saw her I broke down crying and just laid in her arms for what had to be 20 minutes. It was tough because I was looked upon in this situation to be the source of strength.

My coach had left after the draft to head back to his home right outside of College Park, Maryland. The only men left were me and GP and now, just me. ONCE I SAW DEJA, I FELT COMFORT IN KNOWING THAT I COULD FINALLY CRY IN SOMEONE'S ARMS. I soiled her shoulders with some of the most painful but happiest memories of me and my brother.

Days past and the headlines were dominated with arguably one of the saddest stories in the sports news:

"First pick in the NBA Draft, Gerard Penny, was gunned down last night in New York City after an altercation during a robbery in an alley. Penny was 20 and was predicted to be an NBA Legend. Penny leaves behind his mother, Nina Penny and his girlfriend, Alyssa Stone."

His funeral was the saddest event as the entire sanctuary burst out in tears as Gerard Penny laid lifeless in his black casket at the altar of the church. Several NBA and college basketball legends spoke and spoke highly of the resiliency that GP represented and the legacy of manhood that he left behind. To be completely honest, it sounded good and well but I really just wanted my brother back. I wanted to be able to go see him play at the American Airlines Arena. I wanted him to call me after every game and tell about how his game went and I wanted to be there when he scored his first points. I wanted a brother to walk through this dark and scary life with me but that was taken away from me at the hands of a senseless, heartless killer.

Deja was with me every step of the way and she served as a constant reminder that I had to stay strong. She held my hand the entire service and held my hand at the cemetery. That only makes sense to true lovers you see, in us holding hands we exchanged an undeniable energy of comfort between each other. Her palms became my reassurance that although there were clouds in the sky, the sun would soon show its face again.

She also reminded me that it was my job to truly live out GP's legacy of resiliency and strength, insinuating that he now lives through me. About 2 days after GP's homegoing service, NYPD had apprehended the murderer in the case and convicted him of two counts of second-degree murder for the murder of GP and the young lady who got robbed that night. The shooter claimed he had no clue who he had just killed nevertheless, a kill is a kill.

I had my good days after the funeral, but I had my bad days too. Thankfully, Deja was by my side to throw a rope around the sun and drag it into my rainy world every now and then. Truthfully speaking, I was beginning the worst summer of my life and I almost lost my support system in the process.

She almost left me.

Chapter VII
Dusk
7 It's the Darkest

This chapter is dedicated to New York City (Brooklyn), a city who won't stop texting me, even when I'm in another relationship.

August 15th, 2021

A LITTLE OVER a month had passed since the murder of my hero and needless to say, it was the worst month of my life thus far. You never realize how much you love someone until you can't be with him or her every day. GP had really become a fiber in my soul and since his life was taken away from us, there had been a hole in my smile. I couldn't feel myself. I couldn't hear myself. I didn't know who I was anymore and my days had no end, just constant rain and clouded skies.

To make matters worse, our culture has a tendency to create a fabricated realm of over-consideration around death. I mean, for years people continued to flood me with empty remarks of sympathy and smiles that seem like they were built in minutes; then proceed to ask for an autograph or photo. While I appreciated the love, the suffocation from the public made it impossible for my soul to breathe again. The lights never let me grieve the loss of my close friend.

My friends and family suffered in the process and even until this day, I have said a million sorry(s) to them for those dark days. That entire summer they tried to pull me back to my feet because I ate, slept, and lived on my knees for so long. If it weren't for Deja, I would not have finished my senior season. I began a life of eating uncontrollably and living without reckless abandon, losing the core values on which I had built life in recent years. The things that were important to me had lost their value and I had pretty much decided to quit basketball.

I was sitting in my apartment with my front door cracked and the lights dimmed. The darkness became my ally, a place for me to hide from the press and students on my campus. My kitchen counter was covered in empty fast food boxes and beer bottles, barely revealing the tile on the counter. My coffee table was covered in ashes from burned cigars, and my TV was on Cartoon Network with the volume near the lowest it could be. My phone usually rang at least 35 times a day, but I only answered for my mother. Occasionally I would answer for Deja but this particular time I didn't and she had made her way to apartment.

The front door gingerly creaked opened and I heard her soft but stern voice lightly bellow out, "Baby… Are you there?" After I didn't respond, she called out again, "Austin?"

I was drunk and wanted to respond but

my state of inebriation took the life right out of my body and I preferred to sit in silence as the love of life nervously called my name. The door creaked open a little bit more as she began to take footsteps into my messy apartment. I was hunched over on the couch with my hood on and from first glance it may have looked like no one was there. She walked closer to the couch and saw my shoulder before walking around the couch to see if I was awake.

Looking into my blood shot eyes she said, "Austin, didn't you hear me calling you?"

I lifelessly replied, "Yeah, my bad baby. What's up?"

I VIVIDLY REMEMBER THE ENERGY IN THE ROOM GRADUALLY BECOMING MORE TENSE AS TIME PROGRESSED; AN ARGUMENT WAS INEVITABLE AND DEJA WAS GROWING TIRED OF WATCHING ME RUIN MYSELF.

"What's up?" she sarcastically said to me. "What's up? Austin why don't you tell me what's up. [She reached over to turn the television off]. Look at you; you're a mess babe. Please tell me what's up."

The beer sternly spoke for me, "I'll tell you what's not up… You walking into my apartment without my permission."

Perplexed and confused by my answer, her eyes began to water as she couldn't be strong any longer, "Permission? ....Austin, I am worried about you. You won't answer my calls, you won't come out of your room, you won't clean up... [dramatic pause and sobbing] I know.... Things have been.... Rough lately and it's hard without GP, I get it... We all are trying to get through without him but Austin-"

Out of anger I quickly replied, "All? I lost my best friend and you want to come talk to me about how all y'all are dealing with it? You don't know shit about GP, that was my brother. Don't come up in here telling me that you hurting.... I ain't trying to hear that."

I was completely out of character, this was not the usual me. My soft and warm lover, Deja, was being bombarded with so much turmoil. My anger began crippling her soul and it was evident. Tear after tear, I could see the confusion and concern written all over Deja's face. I was not the strong person I was a few months ago and I could tell that it was scaring the love of my life. SHE LOVED ME WITH EVERY OUNCE OF HER BEING AND IT WAS BREAKING HER HEART TO WATCH THE ONE THAT SHE LOVES PRACTICALLY COMMITTING A SLOW SUICIDE.

"Austin, I understand baby…. Please, I just want you to get yourself back up. It's going to be hard but honey…. [pointing and looking around the messy apartment] look at yourself, look around…. Look what is happening to you. This is not what GP would want baby please," she responded in the shakiest of tones.

"You don't know shit about GP," I boldly said to her. I didn't mean it at all but a strong sense of anger and frustration came over me. I was no longer in control of my responses.

Her eyes said it all. She was frightened by the monster that was speaking for me and was in complete disbelief of the way things were going for me. Deep down inside, the sober me was trapped and was screaming for help but on the surface I was a completely different person and this brought nothing but pain to Deja's world. Our unbreakable bond was getting its first true test and our bulletproofed love was taking heavy gunfire.

"Austin, don't talk to me like that," she replied to me in a fearful manor. "I'm only here to help you and you know that baby, I'm trying to be there for you. I want to see things get better for you. You have to do this for GP the right way baby please hear me out," she said to me as she sat next to me on the couch.

I BEGAN TO CRY. FINALLY, IT WAS HAPPENING.

All of the emotions that I wanted to let out over the past month but couldn't because of cameras or just not having the outlet, were coming out. I had been trying to over compensate for my strength recently that I had just bottled up all of my emotions and let it all build up.

She wrapped her arm around me as she began to cry too, pulling me closer to her. I leaned my head on her shoulder and cried every memory I had of GP on her white and red University of Maryland shooting shirt. For the past month or so, I had been holding all of my emotions in trying to be strong for those around me and luckily, she was there to catch my pain.

It all just came out like word vomit; I sobbed my soul into the atmosphere:

"I just.... I just can't believe my best friend is not here with me. All of those good times, all of the times we... we... took on the world man. Why God have to do that? HUH? Why? This man got his life together, why God have to do that Dej? Shit's fucked up."

There was a slight pause as Deja pulled me completely into her arms and allowed me to just cry for a few minutes. Then I continued:

"Baby, he was supposed to change the NBA. He was on his way to being the best basketball player that our generation has seen, he had it all baby. I was so proud of that man. [the sobbing grew significantly more difficult to decipher] We watched him become a man baby, and now he's gone. How could God ever do that?"

Neither Deja nor myself were the most religious of individuals but she certainly leaned on her faith more than I. Her relationship with God was very personal and it was something that she took very serious. Often times when I would get off track, she would be the strong one, rooted in her unshakeable faith.

She didn't take a liking to my questioning of God, pushing me away as my head dangled in defeat. She raised my chin and looked into my drowning eyes and said, "Baby, don't ever question God. He makes no mistakes and I know you can't feel it now, but he is with you." I dropped my head again and continued to cry as the emotions continued to come crashing into my intellect. We sat on my couch in this junky apartment for nearly 5 minutes just holding each other, crying together and letting our exchange of body heat attempt to repair the void in our hearts.

I'll be honest and say that for that moment, I felt refreshed and revitalized. Finally being able to express myself to someone without being judged truly felt invigorating. I was ultimately able to cope with the fact that I would never pass the ball to my number one wingman again; I really felt refreshed to get it all out of my system. That's what made our connection conducive to success and productive to our dreams because we had a connection that not even the most authentic Million Dollar Bill could buy. Our love could literally move mountains and often times, that's what we did.

A few minutes passed and she gently pushed me away again, looking into my eyes with a stern love. Both of our eyes were swimming, I could tell that she wanted to find the words to say to get me back on my feet but the emotion of the atmosphere was getting the best of her. Mumbling she said, "Austin, listen… We are going to get back on track, and… and… turn this around. You are strong, one of the strongest people I know baby, don't lose sight of that."

I nodded my head in agreement as I hung my head again. She pulled my chin up once more and she continued, "This is going to be the best season you've ever had, do it for GP." Something about that sentence struck a nerve, causing me to erupt in anger and say in a dark tone, "I'm not fucking playing basketball again."

Deja looked very confused as her eyes began to gander around as she noticeably began to panic. Dumbfounded and muddled she responded, "Austin, what do you mean? That's not what GP would-"

I didn't even let her finish her sentence before I spewed into a tirade, "Don't talk to me about what GP would want, you don't know anything about him so stop it. [slight pause] I said I'm not playing and that's it."

She replied, "Austin, you're not thinking straight right now. You can't just leave the team-"

I interjected again, "I can do what the hell I want to do, what are you talking about?"

Deja frantically replied, " Austin baby, calm down. Gerard would not want you to waste your talent like this, he would want you to play for him, baby please hear me out."

I got up from the couch and began to pace the room with my mind running 100 miles a minute. Deja then got up from the couch, following behind me in desperate effort to try and calm me down. She tugged on my left shoulder and lightly exclaimed, "Austin, please don't give up on your dream." I turned around to her, infuriated I replied, "Why the hell do you keep mentioning basketball? I told you

I'm done, I don't care about nothing else right now, leave me the fuck alone!"

I had never raised my voice at my Queen like that before. We had gotten into little petty arguments before but nothing to this degree. I could tell that the gravity of my voice shocked every instinct in her body and she was no longer in my presence under an emotion of love but now stands before me in a state of fear. She began to tremble and her eyes began to rain. She looked away from me and muttered, "Maybe I should just go."

I replied,"Yeah, maybe you should. You ain't doing nothing but making things worse right now. "

She replied," Austin, I was only trying to help you, I'm not here to hurt you and you know that, I just wan-"

I replied with even more rage, "Deja, stop talking. Get the hell out of my house and don't come back."

She didn't even respond after that, she simply nodded her head and wiped her crying eyes. She briskly walked to the couch to grab her wallet and walked out of the already cracked front door, leaving it open as she exited.

I watched her leave and as she finally exited the room, I began to clutch my mouth as I knew I had made a mistake. I began to cry once again but this time I was alone. I fell to the floor with my head hung, creating a puddle from the pain that is draining from eyes. I knew I was completely wrong for how I reacted but my mental capacity would not let me react reasonably. I knew that she was only there to help and that she was my rock but I couldn't think clearly because my world finally came crashing down. I had built a support system out of sand to hold my shaken world and finally the waves came crashing against the shore, causing my world to collapse. Deja was the only one strong and loving enough to put my world on her back until it regained its access but now she was gone. LOOKING BACK, I ONLY REACTED THAT WAY TOWARDS HER BECAUSE I WAS SO COMFORTABLE WITH HER THAT

SHE JUST WAS THE VICTIM OF BAD TIMING.

Second after second I would stare at the threshold of my door hoping that she would come running back in saying that she understood the turmoil that my soul was going through; but she never returned.

After a few hours, I picked myself up off of the ground and decided that I was going to announce that I was no longer going to be playing basketball. Coach Donahue had been trying to get in touch with me the last few days, I figured I would give him a call just to let him know my decision before the rest of the team. Still lightly sobbing but mostly gathered, I picked up my smart phone and began to dial Coach Donahue when I had a light knock on the door. My heart jumped, I knew that my lady would come back to me and would be there for me the rest of the way. I knew that looking up and seeing her in the doorway would be the best thing that could possibly happen to me at this point. Anxiously, I looked up into the doorway, excited to grace my eyes with my beautiful Queen. Just then I heard a male voice say, "Austin?" It was Coach Donahue.

"Coach, I was just about to call you," I said to him. Perplexed by the rare and unusual state of my living habitat he said, "Austin, I've been calling you."

"I'm sorry, I've just been… You know," I replied to him.

I could tell from the tone of his voice that he was worried about me. Coach was one of the people I tried to remain strong around. I never wanted to show coach that I was weak or hurt; I always wanted his trust. He walked into my apartment and closed the door behind him. He walked into the kitchen and turned on the light as his alpha personality began to dominate my territory.

"Austin, what's going in here man?" he asked me. I tried so hard to hold everything in and hold it together in his presence, looking down wiping my eyes, I joyously said, "Nothing coach, I've just been a little busy man.... Uh... let me clean up a little bit for you." I hopped up off of my couch and began to pick up around my apartment.

"Austin, stop... Just stop it," he said to me. "What's really going on man?"

As I was picking up around the family room, I paused and took a deep sigh as I looked down at the tan carpet. I could feel myself getting choked up again and the emotions started pouring in again. I broke down and fell to my knees and coach panicked from the kitchen yelling, "Austin!"

He ran over to help me as I once again started crying; needless to say this was a tough day for me. He put his hand on my back and said, "Austin, we all lost our hero and brother. Know that you are not in this alone. You don't have to try and be tough around us, we are your brothers. We're here man, we are here."

I sat on the ground with my head leaning up against the couch.

I didn't respond to him; I just continued to stare at the ground and nodded in agreement with what he was saying. Deja had been the victim of all of my anger in my body and there was none left to distribute among others. The only other emotion left in my body was sheer emptiness.

Coach continued, "Come on Austin, let's go pick up some of the players and go get some food. We are in this together."

I replied, "Coach, I can't be apart of this team anymore." Panicked and perplexed he replied, "Austin, you can't do that. You have too much going for you right now; you can't throw this all away… This isn't how GP would want it and you know that … come on with us and let's get through this."

"Coach please, I love you guys…I really do… but please don't make this harder than what it is." In a very emotional and broken dialect I continued, "Coach, I can't go on anymore and I just really don't want anyone to try and convince me otherwise right now. Just let me work things out on my own coach, please [sobbing], I beg of you."

Coach Donahue disappointedly put his

hand on his forehead in disbelief. "Alright," he said. He patted me on the back gently and continued, "Alright, we'll leave you alone and you don't have to continue to play this sport anymore, you don't have to pursue your passion. Know that my phone is always on and I will always be here for you."

He picked himself up off of the ground and headed back to the kitchen to grab his keys. I sat there in silence as he made his way to the door and just before opening the door he said, "But you know what Austin.. You know GP's last phone conversation was actually about you? All he could talk about was how proud of you he was. I wanted to talk about the draft, and was asking him about how he planned to take the NBA by storm, I even asked about his girlfriend but no, all he could talk about was how proud of his best friend he was. He told me that I had nothing to worry about with him leaving and that this team would be in great hands with you at the helm.... [Pause as Coach smiled a little bit] I'll never forget it, he was so happy... Happy to talk about you, you know? [sarcastic inquisition] It's kind of scary but he said, 'while I'm gone don't worry about anything, I'll be there through Austin.' He really believed in you man. He really did... [slight pause] Just thought I would share that with you."

Coach Donahue exited my apartment and lightly closed the door after him. The room was so silent that the clicking sound from the door closing was the loudest thing inside. So loud that it created a vibration in my spirit that reminded that I literally just kicked everyone out of my life and that I was really in this alone.

I honestly wanted to really take the court and play for GP. I wanted to wear his jersey and I wanted to have the best season ever to honor my best friend. I wanted to take this team to yet another championship and I wanted to marry the love of my life after polishing off yet another NCAA Championship. I wanted to make myself a lottery pick in the next NBA Draft and I wanted to do it all for GP.I just couldn't shake the darkness that came over me. I was ready to let my life perish due to the grips of depression; a sunny day seemed so foreign at this point.

I had kept myself off of Twitter and other forms of social media ever since the horrid New York night but this time, I decided I was going to use Twitter to get my feelings out. I got up and walked over to the couch where my phone was laying. I tweeted a tweet that was felt around the world; A tweet that even until this day, let the entire world down:

"The past few months have been the toughest of my life. I lost my hero & no longer want 2 fight w/out him. I will no longer play bball 4 @TerrapinHoops."

I sent that tweet out, cut my phone off and slid it across the carpet. I walked around the room and turned off all of the lights. I closed my blinds and lit two candles, cracked open another Corona and laid down hoping to not wake up.

Chapter VIII

Dawn

8 From Out of the Shadows

This chapter is dedicated to New York City (Brooklyn), a city who won't stop texting me, even when I'm in another relationship.

September 17th 2021

DAYS MOVED SO slow in the dark. After pushing everything that I held dear to my heart away, my life became a desolate abyss and a playground for depressing emotions. The ones that I pushed away never called me again and I was truly alone under my own wrongdoing.

Everyday for a month I woke up on my back, with my face covered in sorrows. I never opened the blinds, nor did I ever turn on the lights; I simply sat in silence daily. When I went to eat on campus or other administrative visits, I wore a black Maryland Hoops Hoodie (Yes, In the summer) and the same Maryland Flag designed basketball shorts. I had been talking to absolutely no one except my mother; not any of my teammates, coaches, friends or Deja'. I felt lifeless that entire month but deep down inside, I could feel myself wanting to do better.

I was leaving a meeting with my advisor in the Skinner Building on campus, when my phone started vibrating. I nervously reached into my pocket to see who was calling me simply because I didn't want to be bothered. I looked down at my iPhone and saw my mother's gorgeous smile and immediately answered the phone. This was a phone conversation that changed my life.

I answered the phone and heard sobbing through the receiver. Without my mother even saying anything, I could feel the painful torment that she was going through and I immediately asked what was wrong. She assured me that she was worried about my life and the depressing sinkhole that I had fallen into. We had spoke just about everyday for the past month but out of love, she would try to keep me happy during these conversations. She was trying her hardest to conceal her concern for my well-being but I could feel that on this particular phone call, she could no longer hold it in.

MY HEART WAS BREAKING WITH EVERY WORD AND I COULD FEEL HER TEARS FALLING ONTO MY SOUL.

My mother was everything, to me and I felt so guilty for causing her this pain.

I sat down on a wooden bench directly outside the back exit of the building. I listened to everything she said word for word but I specifically remember these words that resonated through out my body:

"You are my hero baby, you made my day brighter. Seeing you on the court used to make me [and your father] so happy. We're worried about you and now I feel helpless. There is a cloud over your head and I can't help but try and fight the rain because I love you, but the winds are getting stronger and we just want to see you still standing after the storm."

All of sudden I was covered with a blanket of guilt and this blanket did the opposite of keep me warm; my soul felt cold as ice. I started to realize the selfishness in my ways, noticing that I wasn't the only person who was counting on me. My entire city and family were depending on me to make them feel invigorated, I was their hope. Then I gave up.

I assured my mother that we would be fine and that I would bounce back from this dark place but I could tell from the tone of her voice she had already lost hope in me. I had already drowned in her tears; a pain that I caused. We exchanged 'I Love You(s) and hung up the phone after a 15-minute conversation. I sat there on the bench, sweating in the September sun with my depressing, black hoodie on thinking about the conversation I just had with my mother.

AT THIS POINT, I WAS SENSITIVE

TO EVERYTHING AROUND ME. I FELT EVERY RAY OF LIGHT FROM THE SUN, I HEARD EVERY CONVERSATION BETWEEN THE RACCOONS ON CAMPUS, AND EVEN ON THIS CLEAR LATE-SUMMER DAY I COULD FEEL THE RAIN COMING FROM DAYS AWAY. My mind began to turn into a theater and my eyes were wide open but they were vacant. I began to see images of my tumultuous past year as they began to flash across my mind. I had flash backs from the brawl at College Park and I felt every emotion of trying to bounce back from that low point. I flashed back to the moment GP and myself held up the Naismith trophy, an image that would go on to be the cover of so many magazines and newspapers. I even re-lived running through New York City with GP and his family getting ready for the draft and then hearing his name called as the first pick, watching his face light up. My mind ventured to us walking that desolate alleyway after the draft and watching vigilance begin to rush GP's body as he attempted to be a hero for a stranger. The trigger pulled and the gun blasted loud enough to make the hairs on my body stand up as I re-lived this moment in my head. I saw the bullet leave the barrel in slow motion, directed towards my best friend. As the first bullet pierced his body,

I woke up. Trembling with fear I dropped my head as one single tear fell from my eye.

I wiped my eye and looked at my phone for a time check as I was in between classes at the time. Noticing that I had a few moments to spare, I decided to head back to the room before my 4:45 lecture class (Which was such a drag, Only class in my life which I hated). I put on my headphones and started walking back to my room as music became an escape for me, allowing me to drown out the rest of the world and my sorrows. For some reason, my mind was louder than my music this time. My troublesome memories were talking louder than Kendrick Lamar and I couldn't drown my brain out. I got to my apartment, stressed out and under pressure I dropped my bag at my front door, took off my headphones and went into the kitchen. With at least 2 hours to spare before my next class, I figured I could take a few shots of liquor to help numb my memory and maybe squeeze in a small nap. I poured a nice double shot of Smirnoff Vodka and then I poured another. It only took about 10 minutes for my sobriety to falter. I jumped on the couch and enjoyed the peaceful bliss of being inebriated and eluding my problems.

I fell into a short slumber before waking for class with the most painful migraine. A throbbing pain kept knocking my pineal gland, causing so much pain that it made it even harder to concentrate. Rushing to grab my things and get ready for class, I grabbed some Ibuprofen (extra strength) and took 4 pills and one more shot on the way out of the door.

I was in my senior year so my workload was heavy but it was mostly big projects in high volume spread out over the year. In other words, I really could have stayed home today and rested up but for some reason I wanted to get out of the house. I walked into class, literally 8 paces before the instructor and pulled out my MacBook laptop ready for class. The students knew me and knew of my trials but they also knew of my personality as of late and how I pretty much avoided conversation with any one. They saved me a seat in the back of the class away from everyone and never uttered a word to me. People had such a respect and sympathy for what I had been through that even my professor never expected me to talk in class.

"Alright guys, happy Friday… We're going to get into the Uh…. Chapter 2 outlook on Life Through the Media but before we begin the Chapter I just wanted to go over a few points that I think would help you," said my Professor to start the class off with. As he was talking, my vision started to blur as my headache only seemed to get worse after taking the medicine. He continued, "I'm going to help make sure every one walks across that -," I began dozing in and out of a sleep-like state as my eyes gained weight at a rapid rate. He continued, "In this Chapter we…." And I couldn't hear the teacher anymore. My eyes had completely shut and I lifelessly dropped onto my desk before falling onto the floor. I don't know what happened next.

I woke up at Doctor's Hospital, staring into the ceiling. The constant beeping of the heart monitor woke me up and served as a steady reminder that everything was not 'Ok'. I was awake but I was afraid to look at anything but the ceiling because I was scared that no one was by my side. I knew that I had pushed everyone away in my life and I knew that I was in this alone. I looked down to my right and saw my parents, sleep on the small love seat like couch. They were cuddled up under a

Univeristy of Maryland blanket; my mother was in my father's arms. The TV was off but I could tell they had been watching it as the remote was not far from my mother. I could also tell that she had been crying as the make up on her face was running down her cheekbones. The pain was painted on her face.

There was a knock at the door that woke everyone up in the room, "It's Dr. Michaels, Can I come in?" said the person at the door. My mother responded for everywhere in the room, "Come in." The Doctor walked in with a clipboard and a folder full of pamphlets. I had no clue what was going on or what had transpired in the last few hours. I was able to see the title on one of the pamphlets, a set of words that I had come to know very well, "Depression & Anxiety".

She asked me, "How are you doing Mr. Arrington? Feeling any pain?" At this point, I honestly didn't know if I could talk or not because I really had no recollection of what could have possibly landed me here. I pointed to my shoulder and my father belted out, "Talk son." I opened my mouth with hopes of being able to talk and I mumbled, "My shoulder hurts a little bit." The doctor assured me that I fell on my shoulder when I fell out of my desk in the classroom. She then asked for my parents to leave the room so she could talk to me alone. Given that I was 21 years old, she had a right to only disclose my medical information to me.

My parents were leaving the room and I said, "Wait, do they have to go?"

Dr. Michaels responded, "They don't have to no, but honestly Austin I would rather talk to you alone for a brief moment before I talk to everyone." My mother assured us that it was 'ok' and that they would be waiting outside. They continued to walk through the threshold of the door and closed the door behind them.

Dr. Michaels pulled up a chair right next to the hospital bed, pressing a button on the side to raise the back of the bed up so that I was sitting up. She sat down and looked me in my eyes with the most sincere and loving smile on her face. It was almost a scary moment because I feared that she was preparing herself to give some horrible news about my health. She took my hand with both of her hands, feeling my pulse rapidly picking up pace due to anxiety.

She said, " Austin, I'm sorry about your friend." I looked away from her, turning my head to stare at the opposite wall. I replied, "Brother." There was a slightly awkward silence in the room before I looked at her and continued, "He was more than a friend, he was my brother." She continued to smile at me, "I know there are a lot of things going through your head right now... A lot of thoughts, a lot of emotions... You're under a lot of pressure Austin."

I dropped my head as she continued holding my hand in this private hospital room. I mumbled, "What happened to me?"

She responded with, " Austin…. You know what happened to you…. I want you to get help, I brought some things for us to take a look at before we talk to your parents." While she began reaching in her pocket I interjected, "Wait, I really don't know what happened to me Doctor, I'm really confused. I want to know what happened! Tell me, I'm sure I can handle it, I promise."

She stopped fumbling with the pamphlets and locked eyes with me again saying, "Austin, you don't have to hide it…. It's just us-." I was growing furious with the confusion and out of frustration I yelled, "Doctor! What happened? I don't know!" She looked into my eyes and saw a genuinely confused young man but also felt the gravity of the pain behind my pupils. The look on my face displayed a sense of sternness that made her drop her head.

Holding my hand even tighter, she said, " Austin, we found 1600 Milligrams of Ibuprofen in your system. [Slight pause as she referenced her chart] And, your blood alcohol level was 1.2."

I mumbled under my breath, " Man, I must have taken too many pain pills." I leaned back up against the hospital bed and let out a disappointed sigh. Dr.

Michaels responded, "Austin, there are better ways to deal with this. I don't want you to hurt yourself, I really want you to take a look at these pamphlets and get help."

I was trying to piece together what she meant or what she was alluding to as to why I needed help. All I did was take too many pain pills and probably shouldn't have been drinking along with it. Then it started to hit me; they think that I tried to kill myself.

"Wait a minute, You think I did this on purpose?" I said to Dr. Michaels. She looked down away from my eyes before slowly saying, " Austin, there are- [pause] places that can help you… I know it's tough-" I didn't let her finish, "Listen, all I did was take too many pain pills, I didn't try and take my life Doctor, and you have to believe me." She sat in silence. The silence caused me to begin to think about the unthinkable.

I already fell from grace in front of the world, I'm sure this had already made national headlines. Media everywhere would have a field day with this story, I began to panic, "Wait, is that what everyone thinks?" I asked Dr. Michaels. She didn't want to answer me but she followed up with her typical answer, "Austin, please let's just,-" I didn't let her finish again.

"I don't need any help! I'm fine! This was an accident!," I yelled at her. She didn't respond. I pulled my hand away from her and asked if she could turn on the television. After a little resistance, she got up and grabbed the remote handing it to me. I immediately turned on the television to ESPN where I feared I was the topic of discussion. Sure enough, I was the headline on Sportscenter and NBA analyst, Gary Greemer and ESPN Anchor, Lindsay Czarniak were set to talk about me within the next segment. My name was on the side of the screen, highlighted under the upcoming topics area. It read, "Arrington Suicide Attempt." My heart dropped.

I started crying and I think Dr. Michaels started to understand that maybe I really didn't try and kill myself. She got up from her chair and came over to hug me, attempting to calm me down. She told me that by regulation she had to send me to another doctor that I would have to report to on a weekly basis but she started to understand that I literally made a mistake and began to apologize. I would be seeing that doctor until the evaluations showed that I was no longer under suicide watch. My parents re-entered the room and we all discussed the entire ordeal, coming to an understanding that I was not suicidal.

It was painful watching news outlets and media outlets talk about me the way they did. Many outlets called me 'weak' or a 'coward', saying that I couldn't deal with the pain of losing my best friend. The saddest truth about the entire thing is that none of these news outlets were sympathetic to GP or his legacy. The story line quickly shifted from "NBA Rookie and First Pick, Gerard Penny, Shot and Killed In New York," to "College Point Guard Attempts Suicide After Losing Best Friend." The things that they were saying about me, tons of unconfirmed inferences, that defamed my character, all pierced my soul. I was none of the things they thought of me; I was just a lost young man trying to find his way. I was not suicidal." Something hit me and caused me to want to prove that to the world that I was strong.

After watching the news talk about my story, I could only imagine the hatred that was online. I had not been on social media in a month since the tweet that ended my college career. I asked my mother for her phone and logged into my social media accounts, only to strike gold. I looked at my mentions and messages only to see that it was covered with an out-pouring of love from everyone across the world. 'Get Better, Arrington,' or 'Oh NO! My Favorite Point Guard is in pain! We love you! #PrayForAustin' were some of the tweets and messages I got online. I felt a genuine wave of appreciation and care as I read everyone's messages online. It healed my broken spirit.

The room was filled with vibrancy as I began to share the love that the world was showing me on the social media outlets. My parents had food in the room that we collectively consumed, passing pieces of chicken while filling the atmosphere with laughter. There was another knock on the door, I yelled, "Come in." The door creaked open and I honestly hoped to see Deja's face. I just knew that she was somewhere hurting without me, watching all of this news coverage about how I tried to take my own life.

The door opened a little bit more and Coach Donahue peaked inside, "Hey family! Can I come in?" We assured him that it was perfectly fine for him to join and he brought some visitors with him. After he walked in, two of my former teammates, Anthony Diskowski from

DeMatha Catholic High School and Dante' Pratt from Rocky Mount Senior High School (North Carolina) walked into the room. Pratt was a Junior Forward and Diskowski was a sophomore shooting guard who had been learning a lot under GP last season, preparing for GP's draft entry. The door still didn't close.

After the players walked in, GP's mother, Nina, walked into the hospital room. My mother jumped up and went to go hug her as they had become friends over the years. My mother then went over to my father and took her with him as they left the room. Once they exited my hospital room, there was a wave of silence. I was filled with all types of life but even deeper, my soul was dreaming again. I wanted to prove to the world that there is a strength that exists that can propel you through some of the darkest valleys of your life. I think everyone could see that look on my face; I think everyone could feel that I was a different person.

Coach Donahue broke the silence, "How you holding up son?" I said, "I'm feeling amazing Coach… I feel strong man." Ms. Nina sat down in the chair closest to me and grabbed my hand, just like Dr. Michaels. She said words to me that gave me the last little charge I needed to get back into gear:

"Austin, I don't want you to say anything to me, I just want you to listen. I love you. I know you didn't try and kill yourself, we all

know that. You don't even have the spirit of a suicidal person right now. I don't know what happened to you but I know I love you. Gerard loves you. The pain you're feeling…. That pain needs to be re-directed and you need to use that to fuel your life. Gerard wants to live through you, I know it baby. He doesn't want to see you on this gurney, he wants to see you up and moving around. How could you know the good times if you never feel the pain? How could you know the value of the sun shining if you never have seen the rain? [Slight pause] You are strong son, the entire world saw that last year. There is a natural champion in you that cannot be bought anywhere. There is a beast in you that can tackle every obstacle. You know, I never told you this but, Gerard looked up to you.

You were his leader and you were his hope. He used to tell us all the time that his brother was his idol. You meant everything to him."

I began to cry as she continued:

"Let that champion out of its cage. Don't let these dark clouds scare away the beast; let that beast terrorize the storm. I don't know what you want to do but whatever it is, be great and know that we are all here for you. Know that GP is here with you at all times. I love you baby."

I told Ms. Nina I loved her as well and we all hugged together. The mood lightened after about 20 minutes and then my parents returned to the room to continue the good times. It's 3 in the morning at this point and we are were still in the room laughing and having a good time; a genuine good time. A nurse had to come to our room several times to tell us to quiet down but if she knew the full circumstances of this entire ordeal she would have been in there laughing too. Everyone was so happy to see me smiling that it was surely worth the disruption of the hospital. I hadn't felt like this since GP was with me.

My mom asked, "Where is Deja? Where is my girl?" My head quickly dropped because I did expect for her to at least come and visit me in the hospital. I replied, "I don't know mom, I thought she would at least come visit." My mother shocked me with her next response, "She did. This is her blanket," holding up the black University of Maryland blanket. "She actually was here the entire time you were sleep and apparently she beat the ambulance here; that's what the nurse said," my mother continued.

I smiled.

I THINK I SMILED BECAUSE DEEP DOWN INSIDE, I KNEW THAT DEJA STILL LOVED ME AND I ALSO KNEW THAT I COULD GET HER BACK.

After a month of zero interaction with someone, you start to question whether or not he or she cares anymore. If she beat the ambulance here, that means she had to skip her 5:00 class (which was ironically in the same building as mine) and hurry down Good Luck Road to the hospital. If she was here the entire time I was knocked out (doped up on medicine), that means she stayed for at least 4 hours. That also means that she probably had to get to work tonight and left after talking with the doctor. This was one big reminder that she in fact still loved me.

I looked up around the silent room and said, "I'm going to get my life back." Everyone looked at me with a sort of joyful look; a look of pure excitement and relief as I was no longer covered in dark emotion but now seemed to be channeling the painful past into a bright future. "Coach, I want to play again. Whatever I have to do, I will do it but I want to play again and we are going to bring another championship to College Park. We're going to do it for GP."

"Say no more, we will take care of everything," Coach said to me as he walked toward me for a hug. Diskowski and Pratt followed him and we all embraced our loving bond, truly proving that we cannot be broken. I made a slight joke, "Well, I guess I have to go ask this damn doctor if I can play since they think I'm suicidal now." The room laughed one of those charity laughs before my mom said, "Yeah, we still need to work on your comedic side." Everyone laughed and went back to their places in the room. My mom then said something else, "Son, you know what else you have to do right?"

I knew what she was referencing, "Yeah, I'm going to get her back mom." I knew that I was going to get my girl back, no matter what it took. She was the angel that God made just for me and only a fool turns down the companionship of an angel. I grabbed my mother's phone once more and replied to thousands of fans online, letting them know that I'm still strong and I also posted that I did not try and take my own life. My last tweet of the night was,"#Back2Back #Terps". I was ready to get my life back and truly live unselfishly; succeeding for those who can't and living for those who had lost that opportunity. GP was living through me and I could feel it.

The dark days were over and my life was back in my control. Pain does not cease to exist but strength does not either, channeling your strength is one the most powerful things you can do. It's the steady hand that you need in order to operate on your future and you cannot let darkness shake your faith.

The next chapter of my life was my strong point; the world was not ready.

6 DAYS LATER ESPN TWEETS:

"BREAKING: PG ARRINGTON RETURNS TO #TERPSBBALL AMID SUICIDE RUMORS. SPORTSCENTER HAS MORE AT 7PM ET/4PM CT"

I was back and I was feeling unbreakable.

Chapter IX
Flight of the Phoenix
9 Soaring Powered By Love

This chapter is dedicated to Rocky Mount, NC; a City where half of my heritage was birthed. Forever a city with reservations in my heart.

October 10, 2011

COACH DONAHUE WAS at the head of the table and the Press Conference was just about to begin. After we received the signal to begin from Dino in the back of the room, Coach Donahue opened the floor:

"Good afternoon ladies and gentleman.

Big season ahead of us, we are glad that you all are here to uh, to be apart of this year and uh, be nosy [talking with hands] about our locker room." The room began to laugh and you could feel the good energy engulfed in the ambience. He continued, "Alright, I'll open things up with a brief synopsis of what's going on with our team and what you can expect from us and then let's take some questions. [slight pause; Donahue puts glasses on and gathers papers] Alright, it's no secret that our team has seen its share of struggles. I mean, we have been you guys' talk of the entire summer, you know? Safe to say we kept you guys in business. [slight snicker from audience]. But you know, [pause] I sit before you as a general who is fully confident in his army. It's no secret, we have seen our share of dark nights, you know? [Pause as emotion builds] We.... [mumbled, starting to whimper] Buried our hero a few months ago [Pause] and uh, we now do everything for him. He is with us today and he will be with us to help drive us through this great season we have coming up. [Long Pause] "

I sat there to the right of Coach Donahue with both Amonti Perry (Now a sophomore) and Darius Pittman (Also a sophomore) seated to coach's left. To my right was an empty chair with GP's jersey sitting in it. We all had name tags to reassure the press of our identity and in front of the empty chair was a name tag that read , 'Gerard "GP" Penny'. When coach began to reach the emotional point of his opening statements, everyone started to look over at the empty chair during the press conference and was whisked away by a boisterous wave of emotion. One of the press members exited the room during Coach Donahue's speech simply because the emotion was so suffocating.

After about 3 minutes, Coach continued, "But I am especially proud of the resiliency of our team, our ability to bounce back and learn how to channel our energy. We have a great team of leaders that GP made sure he cultivated before leaving for the draft; I have nothing but faith in this group. I'm especially proud of this young man to the right of me, [Patting me on the back] Austin Arrington, uh….. The man that he has become will shock you. I'm happy to see him back on his feet, I'm happy to see our entire team back on the battle field and ready for war. Alright, now I'll give you a quick run down of our game plan this year, Austin Arrington will lead our team as our starting Point Guard for his senior season and we have decided to put our Sophomore and top ranked Guard, Amonti Perry along side him. It would be a swift moving offense with those two at the helm, we're going to pick up the pace this year and attack teams within the first few minutes. I expect that under the basket we will continue to be a force to reckoned with as our sophomore big man,

Darius Pittman will be under the basket along with our Junior Power Forward, Dante Pratt and uh, a quick shooter at the Small Forward, Anthony Diskowski. This will be a big year for us; A lot of heart you know? Just feels good. We have a lot of our hero in our soul this year."

Coach continued to talk about the X's and O's, going into detail about our revitalized game plan for this year and talking about our depth on the bench. He spoke for about 20 minutes and he spoke with a fervent gravity in his tone; he believed that we would go back to the National Championship and everyone in the room had no choice but to believe it as well. Coach concluded his monologue and then opened up the room for questions. I knew that the bulk of the questions were going to come my way and many were going to be about the alleged attempted suicide and how I am coping with the loss of my friend. Coach Dino and part of the Press Department of University of Maryland Athletics helped me prepare for these questions so needless to say I was ready. The questions began flying in:

"Jefferey Dawning, Sports Illustrated, this question is for Austin Arrington, [pause for acknowledgement] Austin, how are you feeling?"

This was an easy question; I responded with full confidence in my tone, "Ah man, I'm good! Without question you know, it's been a trying year for us and for myself but I'm good. I've been seeing a counselor, started going to church and uh, been consulting with my family here at Terps Country, So……I'm good now. Thanks for your question."

Another hand went to the sky and a reporter stood up, "Mark Plummer, Austin it's good to see you man." I smiled once I realized who it was and giggling I responded, "Mark, always a pleasure!" Mark continued on with his question, "What really happened that night you overdosed?"

I fired back with a loving but stern tone, "Mark, I'm not trying to get into that man, We're here to talk basketball [Mark takes his seat after being denied an answer]; I'm here and I'm good!"

A couple of questions circled the room, a good majority of them directed at Amonti trying to gauge how prepared he was to try and fill the shoes that GP left behind. It's hard to believe that literally a year ago we were all fighting and now we sit in this press conference together, as one team and with one common goal of carrying out GP's legacy. The press conference went on for about 37 minutes before one last question came my way from Alnese Alexander from the Washington Post, "Austin, is everything together for you? Is your support system still willing to help keep everything together?"

To this day, I think that Ms. Alexander must have known that me and Deja were no longer together and that our relationship had been rocky. I found it quite odd that she would ask me about 'support' system and if you could see the look on her face, it was almost as if she was hinting at something else. In those brief 5 seconds of her asking me those questions, my mind began to take a long journey down memory lane of how Deja impacted my life. I started to think back to first meeting her and how that situation blossomed into a thriving relationship. I even started to think about how she was holding my weak and fragile soul after my best friend lost his life to violence. I STARTED TO HARP ON THE CHEMICAL BOND BETWEEN ME AD MY QUEEN AND REALLY STARTED

TO ZERO IN ON HER ABSENCE FROM MY LIFE.

I answered, " Honestly Alnese, it's not all together but I'm working on it. I have great people in my corner and this team has great support but I am missing something, someone rather, and I won't let it be missing for long. Thank you."

As soon as I answered the question, Dino stepped out onto the stage to wrap up the press conference. I followed Coach Donahue off the stage and all I could think about was holding my lady again. Ironically, Coach pulled me aside and said, "One step at a time Austin. You reclaim your life one step at a time. Go reclaim your lady, she's a good one." I assured Coach Donahue that I had every intention to get her back in my life and I was even honest with him in saying that I would stop at nothing until she was in my corner again.

That night, the team was having what we called a "Black Out Dinner" in the South Campus Dining Hall. It was a tradition that GP started last year where we go into the busy dining hall after the press conference with speakers and music to help us party with the students before getting our season tipped off. It also served as a celebratory event to officially announce our presence as a NCAA Big Ten contender and to make a statement that we will surely make waves in the league this year.

Coach and I walked over to the South Campus Dining Hall, talking about everything from post-graduate life expectancy to keeping me focused during the year. You would have thought we were father and son by the way we were embracing each other. It was at that point that I got to see that Coach Donahue had a deep rooted concern for my well-being and me. He certainly cared about all of his players but for some reason, his roots were deeper in my spirit. Right before we took our steps across the Dining Hall threshold Coach Donahue stopped me and said, "Austin, I was worried about you. GP would be really happy to see you right now. I have to be honest with you, this is not the last time you will have your heart broken by the angel of death. The key is learning how to bounce back and that's what you are doing right now. Know that you are not alone son, and know that you are doing what GP would want you to do right now. This is your team." I nodded my head and stuck my hand out for a handshake and coach shook my hand, pulling me in for a hug. We then walked into the cafeteria with his arm around my shoulder. The room was filled with students showing their support for us by wearing their black and red University of Maryland apparel. Members of the press were on hand with their video camera rolling, ready to make a story out of this emotion stirring night. It's amazing how appealing a story of triumph is.

Walking into the dining hall felt as if it happened in slow motion. Looking around, the building was draped with joy and anticipation, smile after smile, you could feel sustenance. There are very few things in life that could amount to the feeling of true love. It's an emotion that is often times fabricated in many relationships and marriages; that 4-letter word has been taken advantage of and abused for so long. Tonight was dripping with love in its purest form as the dining hall was filled with people who believed in our dream. Looking back on that night, I still say that GP's spirit embodied that entire room and everyone's demons had no choice but to flee.

It felt like everyone on campus was there that night. I really hoped that one person in particular had made her way out there to support my pliability and me. One of our student DJs was playing everyone's favorite party records and while Coach Donahue was in search of a microphone, I was scanning the room hoping to lock eyes with Deja. Looking back, my soul told me that she wasn't too far away from me and that tonight would have to be the night that I laid it all on the line to get my lady back. Everything inside was telling me that I would get the opportunity to win my Queen back; my kingdom isn't the same without her.

Coach Donahue cued the DJ to pause the music as he reached for the microphone to make an announcement in the packed Dining Hall. Now, Coach was always intense but this speech was filled with passion as he attempted to stir the waves to make our seas dangerous for other teams to cross. I continued scanning the room in a desperate search for the love of my life, hoping to cross paths with her. After a few minutes of searching I struck gold, I found my lady. She was walking into the hall with 3 of her friends, gracefully piercing the wind with her confident but gentle presence. Her angelic aura surrounded her curvaceous frame and her smile was the accenting piece, much like a matching handkerchief on a Sunday afternoon ensemble.

THOUSANDS OF CHEERING

BASKETBALL FANS PACKED INTO THIS ROOM AND I WAS IN SEARCH OF THAT ONE. IT WAS ALMOST AS IF EVERYONE IN THE ROOM WAS PAINTED IN BORING, DULL, AND DRY COLORS AND DEJA WAS A COLLECTION OF SOME OF THE RICHEST COLORS IN THE PALETTE.

Coach wrapped up his speech and got the entire building fired up and believing in Terps Basketball again. He then brought me on the microphone [with no warning, might I add], "Alright Terps, I know whose voice you want to hear; I know you want to hear from your general, our leader, one of the strongest voices on our team, Austin Arrington!" The building erupted in applause as I made my way to the microphone. I had no clue what I was going to say to all of these people but I figured that God would give me the words by the time I got to the microphone. Coach handed me the microphone and my heart began to accelerate and my hands began to tremble.

At this point, the words were dancing around in my head and I couldn't catch them. I stood there at the head of the room, just looking out on to the crowd as they continued to cheer for me. Tears started to run down my face and I dropped my head as my teammates came around me to hug and console me. This was going to be a great season; I could feel the energy engulfing my soul as I stood in the heart of my team. After what felt like eternity but in actuality was a few minutes, I put the microphone up to my face as if I was preparing to address the crowd. With shattered dialect and immature courage, I spoke:

"We are still here! [Crowd erupts in praise] We are Terp strong! [More praise, then dies down] It's been a long road for this team; a long couple of months but we have something to prove this year and we're going to stop at nothing until we make history. [Crowd Applause] We lost our hero; our angel earlier this year and it took a lot out of us. Hell, I'll be real and say it took a lot out of me man, I didn't want to go on without him. [Dramatic pause] He was my best friend and I mean, not being able to see him shook me up. Still makes me weak for real. They said I tried to take my own life, that ain't true man I wouldn't do that to GP. But, they want a story so let's give them a story. Let's give them a season that they can talk about and let's hang up another banner in the Comcast Center!"

The crowd continued to cheer and chant as I stood there overlooking everyone in the room. They still looked dry and colorless as I located Deja in the room who's blinding array of colors caught my attention from all the way across the room. I wanted to get her back and at this point I didn't care what anyone else thought and I didn't even care about making a fool out of myself. What I did next, me and Deja talked about it forever. I waited for the crowd to die down before I continued:

"You know, they asked me about last year's success and even my personal success, how did we do it? I would be so foolish to pretend that I did everything on my own with nobody in my corner. Truth be told, I'm nothing. I can't do this. I couldn't lead this team last year by myself. I don't want to spend tonight talking about me but I want to teach this lesson and share this story that a prizefighter is only as good as the people in his corner. The people who rub you when you have been hit; the people who will stop at nothing to heal the wounds that you have acquired after being beat up in the ring of life." I stopped as I could look around and see the puzzled look on everyone's face. They were wondering where I was going with my speech and honestly, I may have killed the mood by talking about something other basketball. That night, I think I fell in love with inspiring people. My goal for this little point in time was to dig inside the minds of others and infiltrate their demons, and deposit some positivity into their spirit. Although I was in love with having that influence, I knew I had to wrap things up soon.

I continued, "I was a wreck this time last year. I didn't get myself together on my own; I had help. I had someone who loved me enough to sweat with me to get my life back on track. She was there every step of the way, one foot at a time. I failed, she failed, and if I succeeded, we succeeded. [Pause as a slow applause started to build] Over the past few months I had become a monster, someone that people couldn't recognize because I began to treat those around me horribly. I pushed her away, but she is here tonight. Deja!" I yelled out. "Deja, I know you are here." I was looking in her general vicinity the entire time and when I began to talk about her she was trying to leave, "Deja, wait... Please stop."

She was trying to leave the dining hall, picking up her pace in the direction of the exit and I could see her friends trying to encourage her to stay and listen. "Deja, just hear me out please," I continued to plead to her over the microphone. She finally stopped after her friends begged her to. I knew that this was my opportunity:

"Dej [pause] , Honey I love you; And I can't do this without you. All of this [pause] All of this you... You make me feel invincible and strong." I completely forgot that the room had other people in it, all I saw was her. Her friends began to clutch her in their arms as she noticeably began to break down. My words combined with my sincere passion were breaking down her walls and she was slowly submerging into her love for me again.

I addressed the crowd:

"You see, she helped me get here. If it wasn't for her, I would have really tried to kill myself that night and it wouldn't have been an accident. If it wasn't for her, I would have never bounced back last year after being benched. [slight pause] If it wasn't for her, I would not have been able to lead this team to a national championship last year. You see, I let this go. I let her go and I shouldn't have. I didn't know how to deal with the pain in my life and in the process, I pushed her away. But, here I am today…. Right now… Saying that I'm sorry and I love you baby, I need you."

The entire room was frozen still as I bared it all on National Television.

Everyone started cheering as the cameras started flashing, trying to capture this moment. University of Maryland had really become the hotbed for some great and entertaining stories. This was definitely one of them. Coach Donahue made his way to the microphone and started to try to rally the students again, "Alright, I'm not coming back up here after that love story, I don't even know –" just as he was talking, Deja interrupted from the crowd, "I Love you too Austin!"

The room was whisked away with applause and all I could think about was running out into the crowd to go and hug my lady. I jumped off of the stage with haste and pushed my way through the crowd trying to get to her. Finally, the unthinkable happened as one of the male students stopped me in my tracks on the way to Deja. He lifted me up and began moving me through the crowd like I was a rock star at a concert. I was officially crowd surfing to get to my girl.

I finally got to her and even though I forgot that the room was filled with other people besides Deja, I remembered they were there now. I could feel every pair of eyes looking at my lady and me, anticipating the big moment that we would embrace. Honestly, I was too. I had not seen her in so long; all I wanted to do was hold her for 1 million moons and 1 million and 1 suns. I can honestly say that I missed her so much that my initial emotion was not sexual at all; it was pure passion and raw love. My heart has not been beating the same after being separated from her heartbeat for so long. I wanted to suffocate in her air, I don't like breathing on my own. Some people didn't understand our relationship and how I never wanted to be alone but a love as deep as ours is such a rarity that more people will dive into the eye of the needle than understand it.

There we were, standing face to face with each other for the first time in a few months. The crowd had circled us and had started chanting, "Love! Love! Love! Love!" I looked into her soul and said with full confidence, "I love you Deja." She replied and said, "I love you too Austin!" She then ran and jumped into my arms as we passionately kissed, reconnecting the broken love. Coach Donahue continued to talk on microphone, "Look at that! We got her back! Let's go Terps!" I honestly think that Coach was surprised and a bit confused about what had just unfolded here at the 'Pep Rally' that he really didn't know what to say. Most people were focused on Deja and myself anyway as they were cheering for us and we kissed in the middle of this crowd.

We left that night and I held her in my arms for 8 hours straight. We didn't move a single muscle and were seemingly attached to each other, joined at the heart, as she rested her head on my pained chest all night long. I stroked her scalp with one hand and with the other massaged her backside as my first and only priority was to allow my love to keep her comfortable and warm.

Hours past and the sun felt like it was minutes away from rising. She had helped me begin this habit of getting up early to go shoot around and surely, I was back on track with everything. I woke up, kissed her on her forehead, my lips embracing her third eye, and got ready to go to the gym. I threw on my University of Maryland Basketball hoodie and shorts, grabbed my lucky basketball and jogged all the way to the Comcast Center.

I walked into the gym with an all new understanding and an all new outlook on life, and a completely new attitude. The lights were dimly lit and the bleachers were completely empty. I sat in the courtside seat, dribbling the basketball between my legs as I sat in the chair. Dribbling the ball back and forth, I knew that I had regained my composure in life and I knew that GP was with me. Nothing could break my spirit at this point and we were headed to yet another historical season. I got up from my chair, looked around the gym, and dribbled my way onto the polished floor, eager to begin a new life.

I WAS FULLY CONVINCED AT THIS POINT THAT WITHOUT DEJA, I AM NOTHING. I KNEW THAT I COULD NEVER LET HER LEAVE ME

AGAIN.

Chapter X

The Angel's Mission

10 She Answered The Call

This chapter is dedicated to SWA Flights 3176 and 2987 whose window seat reminded me of the clouds I dream upon. The altitude served an inspiration to finish the last leg of this composition journey.

March 21st, 2022

WE DOMINATED THE entire league that next season; One by one, we slayed both Goliath and the dwarfs with the same force. We were forceful in our siege but even the successes of athletic dominance were minute to the success of having my angel on the sideline. TO ADD EVEN MORE ROSES TO THE GARDEN, I HAD A PHENOMENAL SUPPORTING CAST BEHIND ME EVERY STEP OF THE WAY; DEJA NEVER MISSED A BEAT.

We played a packed season this year and went a complete 31-0 finishing as the number 1 ranked team in the NCAA. We then put our names in the record books after achieving the impossible feat of beating every opponent in the conference tournament by 15 or more points. This season was unbelievable.

It was an even better season for me as many of accomplishments were more at the core rather than on the surface; personal achievements as opposed to the athletic success. This year was all about the indelible lessons that life taught me as well as the impeccable leadership skills that would echo into my future for decades to come. Statistically I was sound as the starting Point Guard for the Terrapins in my senior year averaging 13.7 PPG (Points Per Game) with an astounding assist rating of 11.2 APG (Assists Per Game). My measly statistical achievements were minor to the amazing season that Amonti Perry had, filling GP's big shoes and averaging 25.6 PPG and 4.9

APG. It was scary and refreshing at the same time being able to play alongside such a vibrant talent like Amonti; very reminiscent of the legend to be, Gerard Penny.

We were the scorers on the team and usually carried our team to victory night in and night out. I became a fearless leader much like a general in the army who chose to lead from the front lines of the brigade. I didn't just give the sport my all; I gave the team my all. I gave GP's legacy everything I had because there was a love in my heart for my best friend that wouldn't let me give anything but my best. I wore GP's #5 jersey that entire year and I wore it with resilience, class, dignity, and love. Going into the national tournament we decided as a team that we were going to wear the Roman numeral number 5 on the back of our shorts, embroidered with the Maryland flag to honor our fallen hero. We were making history not just for him but because of him. His legacy left such a powerful mark on our team that even in his absence we played with and through him. He played through Amonti as well; the hard work and training that the two of them did together in Amonti's freshman year was certainly evident this season.

We made history in the conference championship and now we were ready for selection Sunday to reveal our fate in the National Championship tournament. We were 100% certain we were the number

1 seed; it was just a matter of trying to find out who would be our competition throughout the tournament and where we were supposed to be playing. Coach had decided that it would be of good taste and honor to watch the selection Sunday presentation with all of GP's family in the Comcast Center. We called it "Black Sunday" and handed out black 'Terps' Under Armour shooting shirts with the Roman Numeral '5' on the front. If you looked really closely into the red and yellow color shading in the lettering print, you would notice a collage of images of GP in action. We decided to name the shirt 'Forever Five' and it would be our shooting shirt throughout the entire national tournament. We strategically had

the arena set up so that when fans walked in, they were greeted with a huge 'Thank You' goodie bag from the Basketball Team.

In their seats was a black 'Forever Five' drawstring bag filled with all types of heartfelt giveaways. Taking their seats and opening the bag they would find the 'Black Sunday Forever Five' T- shirt, a black 'Forever Five' water bottle, and a commemorative 'Black Sunday Forever Five' Towel. On the back of the towel was the writing, '#Back2Back' as we were looking to win the championship again all in the name of Gerard Penny. Historically, this season would go down as the 'Forever Five' season and would leave a mark in the basketball hall of fame as one of the greatest college basketball stories in history. The 'Black Sunday' Selection Show event was our way to give back to the faithful fans of College Park who were there with us in the every step of the way as we fought our way back to our feet after losing someone we held near and dear to our hearts.

That morning I woke up alone, throwing a basketball to the sky in a shooting motion as I waited for the sun to rise so I could go to the gym and get my day started. As I continued to wait on the sun, I couldn't help but think about the hero that God blessed me with. All of my life, I had believed in true love but I never experienced it and honestly never thought it would happen. I was always a more reserved and focused person, never really was the one to have a collection of women. The groupies hated me because I would never open up to them and they couldn't have their way. My taste buds were craving the coveted feeling of true love and Deja satisfied my desires with her passionate company. Everyday with her I felt the rays of the sun slowly peeling back the layers of whatever struggles I was battling at the time. As the clouds would move into my life, she was always there, sometimes with an umbrella but sometimes with no umbrella; either way she was there with me every step of the way, bracing the rain and I thanked her everyday for the rest of her life.

I threw the basketball to the sky one last time and hopped up out of my school-issued full size bed. I put on my workout clothes and headed down to the Comcast Center for my typical morning workout. I walked slowly into the gym, looking up to the sky, allowing the energy of the arena to flow through me. The ambience of the arena started to flow through my soul, reminding me that the path of the champion is never perfect but faith in God and the process will guide you through your imperfections. I told coach about my daily shooting rituals and to my surprise he was there sitting courtside with his grey Under Armour T-shirt tucked into his sweatpants. "I'm just here to watch," Coach said to me as I walked into the gym.

One of the 3 other seniors on the team, Michael Drew IV, had been coming to my early morning workouts recently and had just walked into the gym himself. "I see we got company huh," Mike said to me [referring to Coach Donahue].

After shooting around for about 45 minutes, Mike said he had to leave so we wrapped up our workout. Mike shot his last shot and walked out of the gym, I gathered the basketballs and headed for the seats courtside next to coach to put my pants on and change my shoes.

I began untying my shoes and sliding my sweats over top of my shorts. Coach broke the silence by saying, "You going to give me that kind of performance in the tournament?" I assured him by saying,

"C'mon, did I ever let you down?" He laughed lightly to himself and replied, "Well, that is true. You've been starting off your morning like this everyday?"

I replied, "Yes sir. Deja said that if I wanted it, I would have to show it and should put in work every morning." He smiled with a blissful expression and patted me on my back. I could tell that he was proud of me; I could feel the vibe from his smile and the energy of approval in his eyes. It was reminiscent of a father being satisfied with his son's progress. He was the father bear who saw that his son was hungry for success and saw that he no longer had to take me to the lake to fish for food to survive; I'll get up and go myself.

"Let's go get breakfast, my treat, " Coach Donahue said to me. We shut everything down in the gym and looked around one last time at the seats filled with the goodie bags. I think we both had that moment where we felt GP's spirit saying, "Well Done." Coach told me to wait outside and he went on to cut the lights off in the Comcast Center and we walked together to his all black BMW 730 and headed to the College Park Diner for a quick bite to eat. It was certainly a conversation that I would never forget.

Over our omelets and French toast, Coach Donahue told me that he was proud of the man I had become. I let him talk without interruptions as his words were warming to my soul:

"You know Austin, I'm proud of you. Your passion and drive has completely turned your life around; you're really making GP proud. I can just imagine the man you will become in the future."

Coach Donahue had 2 sons; the oldest was 11 and the other was 6. I always felt as though I was his first son as our relationship had grown exponentially over the years to the point where he was no longer my coach but my basketball father. I could tell that I had made him proud and seeing that expression on his face gave me even more encouragement to be a greater man on and off of the court.

Our next piece of conversation shocked

me even more and heartened me to make a decision that changed my life forever.

Coach said, "You know, I am certainly proud of you but I want to warn you about something." A little bit startled I replied, "Yeah, what's up?" Coach said, "Whether we win the championship again or not, I'm happy at the progress we have made. We've become men and we bullied the entire league and showed them our stripes man, that takes some pride; That takes some courage. But I have to be honest with you…. [slight pause] What I really care about has absolutely nothing to do with basketball."

The waitress came over and interrupted our conversation, "Need more syrup?" We denied her sweet offer and Coach continued:

"Yes, I want to raise up that trophy in a few weeks but I care more about my players calling me 10 years from now telling me about their families and good decisions. All of this [referring to the basketball success] means nothing in comparison to being a successful man, [slight pause as he rearranges some of the plates on the table]. None of this holds a candle to being a good family man and being a man of good character."

In my head I'm thinking a mile a second, trying to decipher why he is telling me this. I mean, it was a great monologue but we were two weeks away from winning our second national championship in a row, there were other things to discuss. I mean, we just completed one of the most memorable College Basketball seasons in NCAA History; we were all characters in an amazing sports story but Coach was talking about life with me.

I think he could tell that I was kind of puzzled by his conversation, he said to me, "Did you hear me Austin? You kind of blanked out." I was so busy trying to find out where on earth did this conversation come from that I completely neglected to respond to him. He continued, "Listen, don't let what's important slip away. Don't lose something good, your dreams will unfold as long as you hold on to real love. You hear me?"

I definitely heard what he was saying and

appreciated his words of encouragement.

HIS CONVERSATION OPENED UP A DIFFERENT WORLD FOR ME, BRINGING ME THROUGH THE THRESHOLD OF A DOOR THAT I HAD BEEN BANGING ON FOR 2 YEARS.

Coach got to watch me continue to leap at the ledge of manhood, desiring to be a man through and through, and he was now telling me to finish the course and become a man. He was introducing me to real responsibility, reminding me that life is much more than basketball championships but is also about the life lessons involved. It's more so about surrounding yourself with real love and keeping your loved ones close to your heart than it is about having an unstoppable jumper. He reminded me that once you get your hand on something or someone good, it's important to not let them slip away. He encouraged me to be efficient as a miner for happiness, and truly appreciate the value of the rare jewels I come across in life.

He continued, "You have a good one Austin, don't let her go [in reference to Deja]." I assured him that she was the angel in my life and that I had been soaring on her wings. Her vibrant personality and pure passion for the success of my dreams has elevated me to that point thus far and I would be a fool to let her slip from under my fingers.

I left breakfast with Deja on my mind. We were texting all day that day; I'll never forget it. I feel like I smiled at everything she sent and my mood elevated the minute I saw her name pop up on the front of my phone. She was telling me how excited she was about Black Sunday and how she has been preparing for the media side of things all day. As we were getting closer to graduation, she was really beginning to hone her skills to prepare her for a job post-graduation. Her internship at NBC pretty much solidified her a position pretty much anywhere in the country. Also, her phenomenal job covering the University of Maryland athletics has propelled her to a reputable height in her new career. Keep in mind; she was the first to announce the news that GP was going to the NBA.

We met for lunch after her Broadcast News Writing and Reporting class. Ironically, we went to the same place that was the birthplace for our relationship. She met me near Big Play (a sports bar) and we walked from there to Royal Farms, grabbed 12 pieces of Fried chicken and at least $15 worth of candy. We took our food to the front lawn of the campus and enjoyed our food in the midst of the gorgeous spring weather; a good old-fashioned picnic. There was never a dull moment and I was never happier in my life. We told jokes and made fun of each other putting our unbreakable bond on display for anyone walking by us on campus to see, a display of real love.

She made a comment about my ears (I hate my ears) and I threw a chicken leg at her. She threw a French fry back at me and she got up as if she was trying to run away. I got up and chased my lady around the empty grass area, completely forgetting about everyone else in the world. It felt as if it was just the two of us on the entire planet. It felt like we were two characters in a James Cameron romance, frolicking in the wind scored by the symphony of love. She finally gave up the chase and fell down to her knees a few paces away from the McKeldin Library. I knelt down beside her and turned her around and kissed her as if the sun was drawing closer to earth and our days were numbered. She was the star that I dreamed about day in and day out and she was in my arms.

WE PULLED AWAY FROM EACH OTHER SMILING AND FEELING COMPLETE BLISS.

I can honestly say that at this defining moment, I could look around at the different hallways of my life and be proud of everything. The stars, moon, sun, and earth were all on their axis in my world, everything felt just right and Deja was the magnetic field at the core pulling everything together. She was the right amount of gravity in my world of molecular confusion.

AS I LOOKED AT HER, GAZING INTO HER EYES I SAW FLASHBACKS OF THE PAST TWO YEARS AND THE THINGS THAT WE ACCOMPLISHED TOGETHER. I REPLAYED THE CONVERSATION THAT COACH DONAHUE AND I HAD EARLIER AND EVERYTHING WAS STARTING TO MAKE SENSE.

I had an idea.

I left Deja and went to prepare for the big night. I spent majority of the rest of the day soaking in the energy that had taken over College Park like the plague. The rest of the time, I was running errands trying to plan a big surprise for the evening. Finally, the clock hit 5 o'clock P.M. and it was time for Black Sunday. The selection show started at 6pm so, we wanted to start our ceremony a little before at 5pm to give us time to talk to the fans before and get them excited to finish out the last leg of the 'Forever Five' season.

The ceremony began and the energy was enough to power an entire city on. Coach took the microphone inside the packed Comcast Center and said some words of gratitude to the sold out crowd. The fans were engaging with him and screaming from the top of their lungs! The energy was as electric as a championship game as thousands of fans packed the arena, jumping and chanting with their all black on. Since we were giving back to the students and trying to continue to have a big season, we also had one of the biggest names in hip-hop and R&B perform, Marlon Braggs, right before the selection show started. He didn't do his entire set but the Brooklyn native performed his hit, "Homies Gonna Ride" and the crowd went nuts.

After Braggs performed, I knew that it was my turn to address the crowd:

"Terps! We are going to do it again!" I said to the 'blacked out' crowd. "We fought down yet another tough road and because of you, we are here again. Our team is not

14 deep, it's 40,000 deep because of you and we appreciate you all having our backs! [slight pause for minor applause] All of this in the name of the greatest player to grace this court; [pause] the greatest player to grace the earth; Gerard Penny. [pause for huge applause]. We are going to keep kicking ass on this 'Forever Five' Tour and letting people know that we are on a mission! [pause for big applause]."

I looked all the way up to the very last seat in the 400 section and just let the energy of the crowd sink in. Everyone was on their feet, waving black towels and cheering 'Terps' chants. I glanced over at Coach who was 3 seconds away from tearing up and he nodded his head at me.

I knew what had to be done next.

I continued, "So… I must tell you about my number 1 fan…. [Pause for crowd reaction] Guys, we're all family here, Terps united as one. I want to be completely honest with you and say something that you all know and are probably aware of. I was lost after my friend lost his life last year. To be honest, I did try and kill myself [crowd reaction] last year. No sense in hiding it anymore. We all knew that I was not in a good place mentally and I really just wanted to go be with my best friend. However, an angel came into my life and rescued me from myself. She changed everything about me starting with the way that I saw myself, empowering my mind and my future.

EVERYDAY, REGARDLESS OF HOW I TREATED HER SHE WAS ALWAYS THERE FOR ME AND HAD MY BACK. She came to every practice, even the ones that she wasn't required to come to. She is my best friend and thanks to her, I am no longer afraid to fly. You all know her as the leading lady in the media department for University of Maryland Athletics but I know her because she is nice enough to put me on the back of her angel wings from time to time. She is here tonight; you all make some noise for the beautiful, Deja Barlow. [Crowd applause]."

Deja had no clue what was going on and honestly, I was starting to wonder whether I did as well. She walked out to me at half court, the spot light following her from the bench but her aura was stronger than any man-made light. She walked over kind of covering her face, the light shining on her, outlining her impeccable athletically sexy frame. The closer she got to me, the more I realized how the Lord has blessed me with one of his angels. She was so good to me, that I was able to feel God's love through her. I'll briefly explain: She was so amazing and I couldn't believe that God loved me enough to bless me with her. She is my air and I don't plan on dying soon; I did what had to be done.

She walked out to the floor and hugged me, whispering in my ear, "Austin Honey, what's going on?" As she rested in my arms, the Terps Cheerleaders and Pep Squad had stepped onto the floor behind her. Marlon Braggs began performing his hit song, "Marry My Angel," a song that was huge that year. The lyrics sounded as if I wrote them; every word recanting what true love feels like and the importance of holding on to it.

At this point as Braggs is singing, I think Deja, as well as the crowd, knew what was going on at this point. Deja started to cry profusely and attempted to hide her face from the public. I began to console her as Braggs reached the last line of his song:

"So beautiful when two souls get tangled, I talked to God and he said 'Marry that Angel'."

At that point, Testudo (the mascot) rolled into the arena on a SkyWalk board. He stopped his board at the visitor's bench and walked to Deja and Myself at half-court. He had a gift in his hand. I pushed Deja out of my arms and grabbed her hand saying into the microphone, "Baby, you brought out the best in me. I almost lost my life I mean, as a matter of fact, I did lose my life; but you helped me live again and I'll forever be in debt to you for that. I have been running after you for 2 years now... I have been running from myself, running to the different goals you helped set for me and you know what? I don't want to ever stop running."

Testudo reached into a 'Forever Five' drawstring bag and pulled out a ring case, handing it to me. I dropped down to one knee and said, "Deja Kasey Barlow, you are my angel and I don't want to ever lose you ... [sarcastic pause] again, that is. You keep me running and I don't ever want to stop. I love you. [pause to gather emotion] Deja Kasey Barlow, will you marry me?"

She tried to really get a feel for everything going on, reaching for a tight grip on her emotions to respond to my inquiry. After 10 long seconds she said, 'Yes!'. The crowd erupted in applause as her family walked out on to the court with my family not too far behind. I had spent the latter half of the afternoon preparing for this evening, running around trying to put the pieces together to ensure that the night went flawlessly and that she would have my ring on her finger at the end of the night. I put the bug in Coach's ear shortly after prancing around the College Park Mall (Grassy area where we had our picnic) and I explained that it had to happen that night. After putting together a plan with Coach, I went and cleaned out my savings account in search of an engagement ring. I flew up the beltway and then highway 50 to Bowie Town Center in Bowie, MD, where I found just the perfect ring. To be honest, I completely guessed Deja's ring size and prayed on my way out the door. While I was in search for the ring, Coach Donahue was back at College Park planning out the entire event. As you can see, things worked out quite well and I couldn't have been happier.

After the proposal, the selection show started and the entire arena was swinging their black 'Forever Five' towels around as we waited to hear how our road to championship was going to go. We were the second team to be mentioned being the number 1 seed in the South Division and one of the 4 number 1 seeds in the entire tournament. The other top seeded teams were the speedy and aggressive Ohio State, the veteran team of North Carolina and the young team of Kentucky. Although we wouldn't have to face them until the end, our division of the bracket was arguably the toughest. As the teams were continuously announced we started to notice that the road was not going to be easy for us. Although the open road was dark, we were fully prepared to handle anything along our path; we were ready for another championship.

After the selection show we all went out to eat at Carolina Kitchen not too far from the campus. Of course our family and friends accompanied us there and Deja could not stop smiling the entire night. She was so happy to be able to look down and see 'forever' on her finger, and I was so happy to be able to look at her and see 'forever' too. That night after we ate, I went home and held Deja forever, nearly suffocating her with my appreciation. Right before we went to sleep, she glanced at me with the heaviest of adorations and said, "I love you so damn much, Austin." I knew she meant it because she cursed and she rarely forgets to keep her mouth clean.

She continued, "I'm proud of you for leading this team. I'm proud of you for leading your life." I went on to tell her about how much the team was worried about our competition and the rest of the bracket. I think she could start to see that even though I have been a courageous leader to this point, the levies were beginning to break and zeal was beginning to falter.

She gently put her hand over my mouth as I was talking, interrupting me saying, "The same God who got you here will get you through. You are the best basketball player I know and you are playing for the best team in the world. I've seen what you can do and I know that you will be celebrating your second National Championship [slight pause] Even if I have to come help you." Completely perplexed by how graceful her encouragement filled up my tank, I pulled her close to me and thanked her before kissing her into the purest of oceans; 20,000 leagues beneath sea level and a billion miles above love.

Her words of encouragement carried me through that entire tournament. We put on a show and never asked for an intermission; the University of Maryland Terrapins were on a mission to the moon. Team after team, we obliterated their hopes of being champions stepping on their necks with respect and strength. Finally, we met North Carolina in the Championship and things were a little rough all game long. They were the only team in the nation who could really give us a slight problem in competition. Their team could match our experience and keep up with us up and down the court; we knew this was going to be a difficult feat.

With 2:16 left of the clock in the 1st half of the National Championship, we were down 14 points. I specifically remember walking to the bench during a time out and dropping my head in defeat. I put my towel over my head and looked at the floor so deeply, that you would have thought I was studying the lacquer on the hardwood. I heard a voice from behind me saying, "Keep your head up Austin, GP is watching." Recognizing the voice, I turned around and locked eyes with my fiancé' and best friend, Deja. I didn't respond. I got myself ready to go back in the game and we took things from a 14-point drought to winning the National Championship by 17 points. Our team played a phenomenal second half. To this very day, I feel guilty for not giving the fans a show that year. We apologized for the lack of competition in the game but we had to do what we came to do.

After the game, I kissed Deja for what seemed like a year. We celebrated hard that night after becoming back-to-back National Champions. A lot of things were still up in the air: *Was I going to get drafted? Does any NBA team want to take a chance with the player who tried to commit suicide? Will I be successful without basketball? What was the back up plan?*

These were all viable questions but they weren't valuable. The only question I was worried about got answered a few weeks ago at the Black Sunday Selection Show. The question of, "Will me and Deja be together forever?" was answered already and there wasn't a drop of rain in my kingdom as long as Deja was the Queen on the throne.

She was the Goddess of my seas, able to shift the current of the waves at the snap of her finger. She helped build bridges between the different countries in my soul and she broke a sweat to keep me smiling. She was forever the prize because she was forever my hero. She was the pot of gold at the end of the never-ending rainbow and I never wanted to stop running after her.

Little did I know that this was just the beginning of our love story.

"Alright Austin, I think we'll stop here for today. Get your rest, I'll be back in the morning."

Lord Brian James

FINALE

ABOUT THE AUTHOR

It is said that you can't run away from your calling & at every corner of your life, you will be faced with what you were designed to do. Any glance into the past will help you realize that Brian James, a Media Personality, Blogger, Actor and Dj, is doing what he was designed to do. Born in Alexandria, Virginia, Brian James knew at a young age what his passion was; Communicating. Mixing his passion for communication with his compassionate style and integrity, James would go on to devote his life to redefining a culture and helping to reinvent the soul.

As a young gentleman, Brian would record copies of local radio stations on cassette tapes and then mimic what he heard in the mirror, foreshadowing what was to come in later years. With his parents both efficient in communications and politics, the road was paved for him to begin his career in communications.

"I remember listening to Russ Parr in the morning on the way to school and imagining myself on the radio. Then going home at night with my mother and watching Big Tigger on BET. I knew it was going to happen then! Wasn't sure exactly what, but I knew something was going to happen."

His unique passion for people and harnessing positive energy is what keeps him afloat in this industry. Alongside hard work, diligence, patience and prayer, the passion for people is what got him to where he is today.

Like many other kids, Brian did a little bit of everything growing up. He became fluent in music, learning to read music at age 9 and also played basketball and football all through grade school.

"Man, I knew I was going to the league. I

would watch Emmitt Smith and just know that would be me one day. I thought I was going to be the first person to play basketball and football professionally," but there was something else in the cards for him.

Brian graduated from DeMatha Catholic High School in 2008 with 2 varsity letters and enrolled into Salisbury University beginning his college career. Continuing his football career at Salisbury, Brian played football for the Seagulls and continued to believe in his dream of playing professionally one day. Brian also continued his quest to learn about music, being accepted into Salisbury's prestigious music program as a percussionist and music major. It's safe to assume that Brian had everything on his mind except school and achievement in the classroom.

After never grasping focus on schoolwork, Brian was placed on academic probation and then summoned before the school board to fight for his enrollment after one and a half semesters.

"For some reason, I couldn't focus on school. I didn't care. I would sleep in classes, go to practice, and spend the rest of the night in the cafeteria telling jokes or in bible study. When I got that letter to come to the office of the provost, I knew I had messed up."

Academic probation prohibited him from playing football anymore but also may have been a blessing. Former teammates helped Brian land a job working for campus police while he waited to go before the school board. While working one day, Brian saw the President of the University, Janet Dudley Eschbach, walking across campus and didn't realize that he was moments away from a life changing conversation.

"Knowing my situation and what I was

faced with, I saw her and I saw an opportunity to plead my case and get my life on track. I chased her down and poured my heart out to her on the steps of Holloway Hall. She was cloudy of my situation but I quickly told her what I was going thru and that I may be faced with being asked to leave the institution. I promised her that if I was given a second chance, I will succeed and make this University proud. She believed me and she believed in me. I remained enrolled in the school, still on probation but given a second chance."

While on his quest to bring his grades back to good standings, Brian's close friends became employees of the school radio station (96.3 WXSU). As their workload increased, Brian began to hang around the station more and became enamored at the dream of being on the radio. Brian joined the school radio station (96.3 WXSU) his sophomore year doing a show with his best friends that came in rated at number 1, every semester the show was running. Brian picked up a side hustle combining his love for music with partying, becoming a DJ. Selling his car to buy his first pair of turntables, Brian quickly began learning the ropes as a DJ and began take a lot of events in the Delmarva area and also events in Washington, DC. He began to host concerts and events as well, learning to use his voice and influence for good.

Brian then applied and received the Program Director job transforming the sound of the station into a competing sound in the Del-Mar-Va Market. Generating record breaking amounts of listeners that school has ever recorded, the radio station began grabbing the attention of the entire market. A school station being at competitive heights in a particular market is unheard of and drew the attention of artists, advertisers and his favorite station at home, WKYS.

At a raw age of 19, Brian began interning at DC's #1 station for Hip Hop & RnB , 93.9 WKYS and with some of the greatest personalities in radio such as his mentor, EZ Street.

"I sent an email to one of the biggest personalities in my hometown (DC), EZ Street, and I had no anticipation of receiving a reply. EZ wrote me back within a hour and wanted me to stop by next time I was home. The rest was history. Too thankful for him."

His hard work and persistence kept him around, working in various departments in Radio One learning Programming, Production and Promotions. James spent countless nights at the radio station, making the floor his bed for power naps on numerous occasions. His character and charisma made lasting impressions on

Radio One, developing some of the most influential relationships in his life. Day in and day out, James got to watch some great examples in media and meet some of the most prestigious celebrities.

"I climbed the ladder. I went from 'EZ's Intern' to 'BJ'. I made a mark."

Going back and forth from school to DC, Brian managed to learn how to juggle all of his endeavors successfully. He pledged the Gamma Kappa Chapter of Omega Psi Phi in the Spring of 2011, thus changing his life and outlook on life. Becoming a 'Que' marked with the very principals he lives by today. In May of 2012, Brian graduated with a Bachelor's Degree in Communication, Media Productions concentration and a minor in Music. His diligence and patience landed him a job the day of his graduation ,at the station he interned for, 93.9 WKYS in Washington, DC. Within a month he "cracked the mic" hosting his own radio show for the first time in cooperate radio & thus becoming the youngest Radio Personality in the Washington DC Market & the youngest to do so at WKYS. His first show was seemingly rusty but after a few more times at the plate, James was rewarded with the overnight slot on WKYS, On Air from 1am-6am every morning. His city quickly fell in love with personality and style of radio, keeping him on air in Washington, DC for nearly 3 years before relocating to Buffalo, NY on the People's Station 93.7 WBLK.

Brian, still having a clouded realization of himself, began to really dive into his purpose, focusing on becoming a voice for the generation. His hard work and dedication landed him in several pivotal points and conversations opening up oppurtunities for him to DJ for several big name artists such as Ace Hood, Fabolous, Wale and others. He has hosted big name shows from Kelly Rowland,

Brandy, Wale, Waka Flocka, Miguel and other artists as well.

He began really diving into interviewing artists and celebrity icons in 2011 after chatting with former Redskins' Cornerback, Byron Westbrook. Since then he has sat down with everyone from reality star Karlie Redd, to his good friend, Waka Flocka. But that wasn't enough.

"I got tired of seeing everyone else's interviews and honestly I got tired of seeing everyone else. I want to be the one to use these interviews to create a lifestyle and free a culture of the very things that enslave us now. I want to get these artists, celebrities and icons to say something that will change someone's lives and we can start to see a better world- one mind at a time."

Brian James accepted the night show

position at Western New York's legendary urban station, 93.7 WBLK. There, Brian brought the show to the coveted place of the #1 Rated Night Show in Western, New York, Brian's World and was heard Weekday nights from Buffalo, New York to Toronto, ON, 6p-10p. Brian has accepted a position in Indianapolis at the Mid-West heavyweight station, moving 'Brian's World across country to HOT 96.3 doing Mid-Days, weekdays 10a-3p!

Brian continues to build a new outlook on our culture by way of Broadcasting, Video, and Interviews.

"I'M TRULY THANKFUL FOR WHERE I AM IN LIFE AND THE OPPORTUNITIES THAT I HAVE BEEN BLESSED WITH. I CAN'T GET A GOODNIGHT SLEEP UNTIL OUR CULTURE REGAINS THE STRENGTH IT ONCE HAD. EVERY DAY IS A BLESSING! I'M JUST THANKFUL. IF YOU NEED ME CALL ME."

Made in the USA
Columbia, SC
26 February 2018